NOBLE GUARDIAN

Fire and Snow
Book Two

KHLOE WREN

Books by Khloe Wren

Fire and Snow:
Guardian's Heart
Noble Guardian
Guardian's Shadow (due out Mar '16)
Fierce Guardian (due out Apr '16)

Dragon Warriors:
Enchanting Eilagh
Binding Becky
Claiming Carina
Seducing Skye
Believing Binda

Single Titles:
Fireworks
Jaguar Secrets
Tigers Are Forever
Bad Alpha Anthology
Scarred Perfection
Scandals: Zeck (due out Feb '16)

ISBN: 978-0-9945190-5-4

Cover Credits:
Photographer: Billy Dee Williams of Ab Salute Fotog LLC
Model: Don Allen
Digital Artist: Jay Aheer of Simply Defined Art

Editing Credits:
Editor: Carolyn Depew of Write Right
Proofreader: Ami Deason

Acknowledgements

I've journeyed with depression since I was a young teenager. Writing this book was heart wrenching as Tina suffers as I have over the years.

I can't thank my wonderful husband enough. He not only puts up with me hanging out with all my imaginary friends but helped me proof read and research this one too. My two beautiful girls who keep me grounded and remind me to have fun. My parents who love and accept me even with all my quirks, no matter how bizarre they get.

My author friends, Imogene Nix, Tamsin Baker and Danielle Sevenwaters, who critique my words and support my craziness.

The ladies and men of Erotic Writers Australia. I couldn't have finished this book without Maggie's Nursing knowledge or Kate's Buddhist expertise. The support you all give me, and hopefully I return to you, is so special to me.

Very grateful to Eden Summers, Danielle Belwater, Sam Pope and my Dad for help with the firefighting aspects. And finally, a massive thank you to my editing team again. You rushed this one through for me and made it possible for me to make my unrealistic deadline!

Xo

Khloe

Biography

Khloe Wren grew up in the Adelaide Hills before her parents moved the family to country South Australia when she was a teen. It was there that Khloe followed her father's footsteps and joined the volunteer firefighting service at 18. A few years later, Khloe moved to Melbourne which unfortunately meant she had to give up firefighting but she's always missed it. After a few years living in the big city, she missed the fresh air and space of country living so returned to rural South Australia. Khloe currently lives in the Murraylands with her incredibly patient husband, two strong willed young daughters, an energetic dog and two curious cats.

Khloe has always loved big cats, especially Snow Leopards. So it seemed only natural that when she began writing her first novel after having major surgery that left her on bedrest for six months, that she chose these beautiful creatures as her first shifters.

Glossary

Alpha (of a Leap): The leader of the Leap.

Continental Leap: The Leap chosen to represent their continent at the Council of Alphas. Each of the seven continents has a Continental Leap.

Council of Alphas: The Alpha of each Continental Leap form the Council of Alphas. It is their job to oversee all aspects of shifter life.

Dream Bonding: After the female turns twenty-one, shifter pairs can pull each other into a dream. Useful for when mates are apart from each other.

Chaton: French for kitten.

Comet Shifters: Those shifters newly created from Halley's Comet's passing of Earth.

David Jones: Large department store.

Firie/Firies/Firie's: Nickname for a firefighter

Halley's Comet: When the shifters were first created. Halley's Comet passed as the magic was welded. Now, every seventy-five years when the comet passes over Earth, a new pair of shifters is conceived on each continent.

Jaws of Life: Apparatus Firefighters use to cut open crashed vehicles in order to save the occupants

Leap: Leap is the name given to a group of Snow Leopards.

Lost Ones: Shifters who are not part of a Leap and often don't know of their heritage. Lost Ones are often alone and scared of what they are, not understanding there are others like them.

Maman: French for Mum/Mom

Marking, The: After mating, the couple mark each other with permanent scratch marks to show their claim on the other. The mark looks like four wide scratch marks that reveal Snow Leopard spots beneath.

Mating: The process a couple goes through to bind themselves together for life. Mating forms an unbreakable bond.

Ma chère: French endearment, my dear.

Mon amour: French endearment, my love.

Petit fille: French for little girl/daughter

Search, The: On of the Council of Alphas' main purposes is to go looking for Lost Ones and Comet Shifters.

Shifter Magic: Because shifters were created with magic, they hold a low level of magic which they can weld on occasion.

Tibetan Monks: Tibetan Monks are the ones who originally cast the magic to bind a man and a Snow Leopard together.

Trigger: Trigger Corporation is the enemy to the shifters.

Ute: Similar to an American Pickup Truck

Widow Mate: Mate of a shifter who has died. Once their mate dies, they are free to find love again if they choose to.

Dedication

To my parents:

Thank you for your endless support and love.

Prologue

Sydney, New South Wales, Australia
17ᵗʰ June 2012

With the AIS Gymnastics Hall filled to capacity for the final Olympic Nomination Trials, Tina Anderson stood before her mother wearing her brand new long sleeve leotard in the Tasmanian team colors of navy and red. Her stomach ached from the butterflies buzzing inside. More nervous than she'd ever been, she believed this was her final chance to compete in the Olympics. No one had said anything to her, but she knew. She was twenty years old and in this game, that was closing in on being ancient for a competitor at these high levels.

Closing her eyes for a moment, she blew out a breath. She knew her routine, was sure she could do it. But in front of so many people, the prospect of failing was a crushing weight pressing down on her. Tina ran her trembling fingers over her head, checking that her bun was still secure and every strand of hair was slicked back where it should be. As she did, she glanced up at her mother. Ms Gloria Anderson stood proud, her bleached blond hair perfectly styled and her makeup flawless. The fitted low cut blouse showed off every inch of cleavage her pushup bra provided. Her tailored charcoal grey suit pants altered in just the right way to show off the curve of her hips. A small smirk curved Tina's lips, as the three-inch stiletto heels really did look out of place down on the floor.

A wave of cold flowed through her as she watched her mother raise her hands to check that her own hair was all in place. Focusing on her face, Tina held her breath as she searched her mother's expression for some reassurance. But all she saw was expectation. No love, no kindness, only ice cold determination and expectation.

The same as always.

It had been years since Tina had realized her mother enjoyed living through her. Loved the glory of being able to brag about her daughter's accomplishments. When she'd found out Tina had made the Olympic Trials, she'd thrown a huge party to make sure everyone knew. Not that Tina had minded the party, she'd enjoyed every moment of it.

"Okay Tina, you're up next. Do me proud and leave them all dead in the water."

The words her mother spoke were encouraging enough, but Tina's heart ached at the flat, serious tone her mother used. Over the last few months Tina had started to wonder if her mother loved her at all, or if she only loved her accomplishments.

Before she could get too buried in that depressing train of thought, the announcer's deep booming voice came over the PA system announcing she was up at the uneven bars. Blowing out a breath, she walked towards the platform, stopping briefly at the bowl of chalk to dust her hands and check her wrist grips before she stood at the starting position in front of the apparatus. She closed her eyes and took a couple of deep breaths while she mentally ran through her routine one last time and gave herself a little pep talk.

I can do this, I've been training since I was eight years old; I know this routine by heart.

When the buzzer sounded, adrenalin flooded her system as she stepped forward and bowed to the judges. Tina confidently jumped, grabbing hold of the lower bar to swing herself up to start her routine.

The coolness of the bar felt good against her skin, the familiar sensation of her flesh sliding around the smooth surface grounding her. A lightness filled her chest as her body moved precisely and smoothly. Her kip and hip circles were perfect and her Stalder flawless. She spun around the upper bar in a Backward Giant, before she let go with her right hand and flipped herself over. She grabbed at the bar with her right hand, but missed. A gasp tore from her throat when her left hand slipped and she found herself adrift, desperately reaching for the upper bar. Panic rose as she tried to focus over the racing heartbeat pounding in her ears, desperately trying to think of something she could do to save herself.

The lower bar connected with her left thigh with a loud crack, accompanied by a level of pain more intense than any she had ever experienced before. With a grunt, she landed on the soft floor mats as spots swam before her eyes, blurring the faces of her coach and team mates crowded around her. As her vision began to dim, she desperately searched for her mother's face but was unable to find it before the darkness won.

As Tina broke through the surface of consciousness, she was greeted with enough pain to make her stomach churn and her mother's voice, raised and angry.

"You need to come and get her." Pause. "I don't care. My life doesn't have room for this in it." Pause. "Yes, just like I didn't have room for you in it all those years ago." Pause. "So help me, Dale, if you don't get your ass up here to collect her, I'll be dropping her off at your doorstep."

She didn't want to open her eyes. The cold light of day would make everything more real. Even with them closed, tears left a cold trail from her eye to where they landed in her ear and the ache in her heart eclipsed the pain in her leg. From the pauses she guessed her mother was on the phone, and from the words spoken, her mother was dumping her on her father, a man she hadn't seen in over four years.

Dale Anderson had always been kind to her. Every year he dutifully posted presents and rang for both her birthday and Christmas, but that was about it. Whenever

Tina had asked him why, he would tell her that he'd love to ring more often but couldn't. He would always refuse to elaborate on why. He'd told her she could ring him whenever she wanted, and as long as he wasn't offshore on a rig he'd always answer her. She'd tried a few times, only to discover that her mother had somehow managed to have his number barred from both her mobile and the house phone. She'd always felt guilty over her parents breaking up. Whenever she'd thought back over those years surrounding her parents' divorce, she'd always drawn the conclusion that it had been the stress of being apart. How could a marriage work with when the wife and child were in Sydney, while the father remained in Tasmania? But maybe that hadn't been right. From what she'd just overheard, her mother would have left him regardless.

Tina's heart rate raced from the anger coursing through her and she was unable to force her eyes to stay shut any longer. Blinking them open, she squinted against the harsh florescent light and groaned.

"Oh, you're awake, sweetie."

Her syrupy sweet voice fed Tina's fury.

"How dare you."

Her mother's eyes widened before she blinked with feigned innocence.

"How dare I what?"

"Call me 'sweetie' after what you just said to Dad. And don't try to deny it, I heard you."

Tina's temper rose higher as her mother's mouth

opened and closed. Obviously she was searching for a plausible lie.

"Don't bother with a response, mother. The look on your face says it all. Why don't you just go? I know you have so many more pressing engagements on your schedule than comforting your only daughter. I'm sure Dad will be here just as soon as he can get a flight, wouldn't you say?"

"I never said-"

With a tone laced in ice, she cut off her mother. "Get. Out."

Tears burned her eyes but she refused to allow them to fall so long as her mother was there to witness them. Straightening her spine and brushing imaginary creases from her shirt, Gloria slung her handbag over her shoulder before heading to the door.

"Well, I do have the party over at the Wilson's tonight. I'll tell them how sorry you are that you are unable to make it. Goodbye, Tina."

The second her mother strode from the room, Tina squeezed her eyes shut as tears leaked out. Behind her closed lids, her accident played like a movie, bringing her focus back from her mother and onto why she was in a hospital to begin with.

My leg!

In a panic she opened her eyes and twisted her head to the side to look down her body. Her left leg was encased in a weird metal contraption which started at her waist. There were long rods running down the length of her left leg to below her knee. What truly had her blood running cold were the pins. Thick metal pins attached to the rods disappeared into the bandages on her thigh. She had a horrible feeling those pins were attached to her femur, probably holding the thing together.

Tina had no control over the great heaving sobs that racked her body. Certainly her career in gymnastics was over now, and so was her mother's use for her. Understanding of why her mother had been so quick to abandon her slammed into her. There would be no more medals or awards for her mother to brag about. Despite her suspicions, it still made her heart ache to have it confirmed that her mother had been living through Tina's accomplishments, relishing the glory of being the mother of an elite athlete.

A torrent of emotions overwhelmed Tina, and her body shook under the pressure of them. Pain from her leg shot up her spine in protest of her body's movements, but she couldn't stop the tears. Tina buried her face in her hands as she tried to deal with the fact her entire life would have to completely change now. As she cried, she stupidly craved the loving embrace of her mother, but she wasn't there, and probably never would be again. A fresh stab of agony sliced her heart and bruised her soul. Wounds which left the pain in her leg in the dust.

Her tears slowed when she felt a warm hand rubbing her shoulder and upper arm. A soft calming voice spoke kindly to her.

"Tina? Honey? Are you in pain? Can you tell me

what's wrong?"

Tina lowered her hands as she stopped crying and started hiccupping through the last few tremors. She looked up into a lovely round face. A nurse stood over her with an expression filled with worry, concern and compassion. Kind of what she had expected—wanted—to see in her mother's face.

"My leg hurts." *Not half as much as my heart bleeding out, but no drug is going to fix that.*

The nurse smiled kindly at her. "The doctor will be in shortly to do some tests and explain to you anything you want to know. But in the meantime, I'll give you another shot of morphine for the pain."

Tina relaxed back into the bed as the nurse injected the drug into her chest port. She welcomed the numbness it brought on. The pain in her leg eased and her mind became fuzzy. Allowing herself to fully fall under the morphine's effect, she drifted off to a dreamless sleep.

Dale hung his phone up with a frustrated growl. He was sick to death of his ex-wife. Days like today, he really wanted to wring her neck. Their daughter would possibly never walk again with her injuries and all she cared about was getting back to her damn social life. Thankfully he was on his two-weeks-off rotation, so he was home and could make the trip up to Sydney to collect his daughter as soon as he could get a flight.

Shit, he hadn't seen Tina in what? Nearly five years? When Tina had won the state championship in gymnastics, Gloria had decided to take her to Sydney to further her *career*. Dale had not agreed. Sure, he was proud of his little girl, but at fifteen she didn't need a career. She needed to be a teenager. Have fun, enjoy being with friends.

But he had loved Gloria and Tina, and wanting to see them happy, he gave in. Working oil rigs out in Bass Strait meant it made sense for him to stay behind in Tasmania while they went off to Sydney. Soon after, once it was clear that Tina was going to go far with her gymnastics, he'd received the paperwork announcing their separation.

His heart had shattered that day.

He hadn't realized Gloria had been so unhappy with him. He'd tried to ring her but she refused his calls. She even refused him contact with Tina. Twelve months later the divorce papers came. It had felt like a blowtorch to his chest when he'd signed those damn things. Being off-shore on the oil rig so much meant he didn't have a chance at fighting for custody so he'd signed that over too, although he had made sure the court orders contained phone call provisions. He could ring Tina on her birthday and Christmas and there was nothing Gloria could do about it. The damn woman had already proven she'd never let him have any contact without the court's say so.

It was now clear as day that Gloria didn't love their daughter any more than she'd loved him. He'd fallen in love with Gloria the first time he'd seen her in high school. She'd loved that he was the best footballer and was the best looking bloke there. Apparently that'd been all she'd loved. He chuckled humorlessly. She'd certainly been aptly named, because Gloria had always been all about the glory.

My poor little sweet pea.

She must be scared and hurting so much to learn her mother didn't care when she needed her most.

He rang the airport and booked the first available flight, then snatched his suitcase from the floor in his walk-in-closet. As he packed, he dialed the hospital to speak with Tina's doctor. He wanted a clear picture of his daughter's injuries from a medical professional, not his selfish ex-wife.

After he hung up he immediately dialed again. This time he rang his boss, Greg. From what her doctor had said, it was going to take more than two weeks to move Tina, and for her to settle in here in Tasmania. Greg was very sympathetic to the situation and told Dale to take as much time as he needed, just give him a call when he was ready to come back. With a heavy heart, he put his phone on to charge. Something about Greg's tight tone had him thinking getting back on the rig wasn't going to be that simple. But it didn't matter, Tina needed him and he vowed he would never let his little girl down again.

It was probably going to be at least a few weeks before he could bring her home from the hospital, and she'd be in a wheelchair for some time. The doctor had warned him she might need it permanently. He could only imagine how Tina was coping with it all. The absolute best case scenario still never had her going back to competition level gymnastics. As he finished packing, he thought about all the changes he was going to have to make. He couldn't afford to not work for long unfortunately, so a nurse or caretaker of some kind was going to be needed, at least until she learned how to care for herself and move around in her wheelchair. Damn, the wheelchair. His house was going to need some major renovating to accommodate it. He didn't mind doing anything required to keep his daughter happy, he just worried about accomplishing it all in time. Especially without him here to supervise it all being done. Maybe he could ring around to a few of his old friends and have one of them oversee the renovations while he was in Sydney. For starters, the bathroom and front steps would have to be done before Tina could move in.

"Was that Dale Anderson's car that just went racing past for the third time today?"

Robyn looked up from the appointment book at Barbara, her friend and employee.

"What kind of car was it?"

"Black dual cab Toyota Hilux—that's his car isn't it? He sure looked like he was in a hurry too."

"That's his car all right. Wonder what's happened..." Robyn let her voice trail off as she thought about what would have Dale in such a spin.

The elderly lady sitting in front of Barbara, getting her

hair permed, spoke up.

"Oh, you haven't heard the news? Poor man."

Robyn gritted her teeth to ward off the sudden desire to throttle the woman. Why did little old ladies have to gossip? Couldn't they just spit the information out already?

"Don't tease, Doris. If you know something, please, do tell." Barbara coaxed.

A sneer curved Robyn's lips. While Robyn would have simply fisted Doris' hair and demanded the information, Barbara gently reprimanded the woman while she requested the story. *Whatever*. So long as it worked.

"Dale's daughter, Tina, had an accident at the Olympic Trials. The word is she might never walk again," Doris let out a decidedly non-ladylike snort of disgust before continuing, "and that hussy, Gloria, just left her. Poor girl. Fancy your own mother walking away from you without a care when you need her most. Apparently Gloria rang Dale earlier today, ordering him to come get Tina. No doubt she had to rush off to get her nails done or some such rubbish. Naturally, Dale is rushing around to get things organized before he flies out to go get his daughter. He was always a good man. Too good for the likes of Gloria."

"What kind of things does he need to organize?" Robyn's mind was working overtime. She had always fancied Dale but had never been able to catch his eye. This may well be her opportunity to get in with the man.

"Well, he's going to need to renovate his place quick smart. No way can a wheelchair get up those front steps of his, for starters. I believe he's also looking for a caretaker for Tina, for when he has to go back out working those rigs of his. Just until Tina learns how to cope on her own, I'm sure." Doris sighed loudly. "Only twenty years old and having to learn how to live in a wheelchair. So sad."

That got Robyn thinking, she was no renovator but she could be a caretaker. How hard could a grown woman be to look after? She'd better get in quick before someone else offered.

"I'm just heading out for a bit. You're all right to handle things for a while, Barbara?"

"Sure thing, boss." Barbara flashed her a wink, indicating she knew full well what Robyn was thinking.

As soon as Robyn was out the back door, she was dialing Dale's number. A number she'd pinched from Gloria's phone many years ago, but never had the courage to use. He picked up on the third ring. "Hey, Dale here. Who's this?"

"Hi Dale, it's Robyn. Robyn Taylor. We went to school together. Don't know if you remember me or not?"

"Sure I remember you. What can I do for you?"

"Well, it's more what I can do for you. I heard about your daughter's unfortunate accident and wanted to offer my services in caring for Tina."

"Oh, um, great. That would be a big help. Do you

have experience with this kind of thing?"

"Nothing professional, but I used to help with my cousin. He's been in a chair his whole life."

She didn't tell him that her contribution to caring for him had been to bitch and moan about having to put up with him to her mother, who was the one who had to actually look after the brat every time her aunt had needed a break.

"Ah, okay. Well, I'm guessing Tina won't need a lot of help anyway. I'm not going to be able to stay off the rigs for very long unfortunately, so she'll need help with her rehab stuff and maybe a little with getting around, that type of thing. Do you think you'll be right with that?"

"I'm sure Tina and I will get along just fine."

"Yeah, sure. Look, I'm under the pump at the moment and need to get moving. I'm not sure when I'll need you to start. Can I get back to you once I return with Tina?"

"Sure Dale, take your time. There's no rush. I'll text through my details and wait for you to call me."

"Great, thanks Robyn. We'll talk soon. Bye."

"See ya, Dale."

Robyn hit the end-call button on her phone as a big grin spread across her face and butterflies took flight in her belly. Finally, Dale had noticed her and she would never be stuck in Gloria's shadow ever again.

All she had to do was keep his daughter reliant on her.

Chapter One

Rosebery, Tasmania, Australia
1 September 2012
The hollowness in Tina's chest seemed to be increasing each day, depression sucking her further down into a deep dark pit of despair. Two weeks ago, on the two month anniversary of her accident, her nightmares had started getting worse. They were now plaguing her sleep every night. When she closed her eyes, all she saw was either the last moments of her routine and felt the pain as her leg broke, or she relived watching her mother walk out of her hospital room and her life. She wasn't sure which hurt more; never being able to do gymnastics again or her mother proving how much she didn't love her.

Tina rubbed her thigh as she recalled the feel of it cracking against the bar. The remembered agony momentarily stole her breath. The doctors had confirmed she'd basically shattered her femur along with cracking her pelvis, and the injury was severe enough to have her living in a wheelchair, for a while at least. They'd said once the bones healed and with time and rehab she *should* get back the full use of her leg, although she would forever limp, and never have the range of movement in her hip she'd had prior to the accident. Thanks to all her years of gymnastics, she'd had great flexibility.

Every morning when she woke she would put all her energy into moving her leg, but on her own she couldn't do much. It didn't help she'd only been shown the exercises a couple of times and struggled to recall precisely how she should do them. Robyn was supposed to be helping her with them but she never did. Her dad might pay her to be Tina's 'caretaker' but she was pretty lousy at it. Robyn was also a real mean bitch when she wanted to be, so Tina tried to stay on her good side. After all, without Robyn, Tina would be housebound.

She tipped her head back to stare at the ceiling.

"How the hell did I end up here?"

Her life wasn't her own, and there wasn't anything much she could do about it. Confined to a wheelchair, she was unable to do so many everyday things for herself. Being stuck with a harsh evil bitch that she was forced to rely on didn't help matters.

Her father had taken leave from his engineering job on the oil rig out in Bass Strait when she had her accident. One month later, when his savings started running low, he'd rung to go back to work but there were no jobs available. His old boss had heard about work going out on the rigs in the Middle East. It was great money, but the only position open had been a twelve month contract. He wasn't due back for another eleven months. Which meant not only would he miss Christmas, but he'd also miss her twenty-first birthday.

Even though she hadn't seen much of her dad in the last five years, the two months they'd spent together before he had to go back to work had been great. He'd been mostly busy renovating the house around her, but she'd sit and chat with him while he did his work. Life hadn't seemed so bad with her dad around, cracking jokes and calling her his sweet pea. She loved her dad, and he made sure he told her every day that he loved her.

So unlike her mother.

Tina couldn't for the life of her work out why her mother had left him. He was a hard worker, still good looking, with his short brown-blond hair and trimmed beard, and he treated everyone in his life well. Her mother must truly be mad to have left him. Then again, the woman did abandon her only child in the midst of a crisis—and didn't that just say it all. Tina briefly wondered what her mother was doing with herself now, before she released a huff as she shook her head. She wouldn't allow herself to care what her mother was up to.

Tina came back to the present as she lowered her head to look back at the computer screen in front of her. Within days of entering Robyn's care, she'd declared Tina needed something to fill her time, so Robyn had shown her how to do the salon's bookwork. Tina had always liked working with numbers. She'd topped her math class the whole way through school, so doing the bookwork didn't bother her. The fact Robyn didn't pay her for it, now that bothered her a great deal.

Rolling the mouse to wake the screen up, she stared at the home page of the accounting software with a sigh. She needed to head out to the front desk to grab yesterday's receipts. Robyn always forgot to bring them out for her, but got shitty with her if she caught Tina out front. Tugging on her fingerless gloves making sure the padded palms were where they needed to be, she began wheeling herself out to the front desk. She didn't pay any attention to what was going on around her. There was no need. Robyn and Barbara simply ignored her existence unless they wanted her to do something, and she didn't want to focus on the happy customers going about their day. She was on her way back to the office with the receipts, wheeling past the front door when it burst open and a man came barreling in, nearly plowing right into her chair. Her muscles tensed and her heart sped up in fear. Without raising her head, she quickly apologized and tried to wheel away before Robyn noticed.

"What on earth do you think you are doing out here, Tina?" Robyn's high pitched voice grated over her nerves. With a long exhale, Tina looked up as Robyn approached her. She knew better than to try and defend herself. Robyn would never listen.

Tina turned her gaze from Robyn to see who had

come in. Her breath froze in her chest. The man was gorgeous. He had to be at least six feet two, with ink black hair that was long enough to look shaggy in a cool, designer kind of way. His eyes, framed with dark lashes, were blue with grey specks and they were focused on her with a scorching intensity that left her feeling a little lightheaded. A twitch of his lips drew her attention to the most kissable mouth she'd ever laid eyes on. This hunk put to shame any other man she'd ever seen before, even the pretty-boy athletes she used to date in Sydney.

"Tina, leave young Mr White alone! You know better than to talk to customers. Now return out the back this instant and get on with those books like you should be doing. They won't do themselves, you know." Robyn grabbed Tina's chair and quickly wheeled her out of the man's sight. She rubbed her palms over her arms, trying to understand what had just happened. Before Robyn had separated them, there'd been a strange kind of energy sizzling between her and the hot stranger. Once they were behind the back curtain, Robyn gave her another mouthful of choice words, which Tina really didn't care about enough to listen to. As always, she politely smiled until Robyn was finished, and sighed with relief when the woman returned to the salon, leaving her alone.

Tina peeked around the door frame to watch as Robyn headed over to the man, who had moved quite close to the curtain. Had he heard Robyn's abusive words? He didn't look happy with Robyn. When he spoke, his deep growly voice slid straight down her spine and lit up internal body parts she'd thought no longer worked.

"Who was that girl? Why is she in a wheelchair?" Tina could see Robyn trying to stare the man down.

"Tina is no one you need to concern yourself with, Mr White. Now I believe your mother, future sister-in-law and niece are ready to go." Robyn marched off toward two women and a child. The small group had arrived hours earlier, obviously here to get beautified for a wedding. The man trailed behind Robyn, almost as though he didn't want to.

Tina turned away, wheeling her chair across the room, tears flowing down her cheeks as she struggled to contain her grief and sadness. She would never be getting married. She would never be getting with a guy like 'young Mr White' either. With next to no movement in her hip joint, sex had kind of lost its appeal. Until now. Mr White held her attention and heated her up like no other man ever had. But what young, healthy good-looking guy wanted a wheelchair bound girlfriend?

Robyn was frowning as she stood behind the front counter looking out after the group that had just left the salon. The way Conner had watched Tina was straight up trouble. Robyn couldn't allow Tina to get involved with any man. He would woo her and steal her away from Robyn's care. She needed to keep Tina under her thumb. It was the only way she could stay in Dale's life. All the plans Robyn had when she took the job of Tina's caretaker were not panning out. Dale was supposed to see Robyn looking after Tina and fall at her feet in gratitude. But Dale continued in his failure to notice her as anything other than the hired help. The only letters that ever came from him were for Tina. To add insult to injury, Tina looked exactly like her damn mother. That long straight white-blond hair, athletically toned body and perfect face. So different from her long dark brown wavy hair, lush breasts, hourglass physique and above average height.

Robyn's mind tripped back in time. She and Gloria had been best friends since grade four in primary school. They'd been the best looking girls in their class. They got top scores in all their classes just by batting their eyelids. Those were the days. But things had changed that first year of high school. From the first second Robyn saw Dale, she'd wanted him. He was tall and buff, and he strolled around the school like he owned it. Gloria never really noticed him, but he'd certainly noticed her. Every time Robyn was watching Dale, Dale was watching Gloria. It hadn't taken long for Gloria to catch on to both Robyn's interest in Dale, and his in Gloria. The bitch had gone after Dale like a bull at a gate. *Bitch*. They'd dated the whole way through school, and when Dale knocked Gloria up end of senior year, he'd married her.

Even though Robyn hated Gloria for her betrayal, she remained her friend after the wedding, just so she could still see Dale.

"I am so pathetic." She muttered under her breath.

Gloria had been so busy showing off her 'trophy

husband' she hadn't noticed Robyn's distaste for her. Then once she grew big with pregnancy, Gloria was too busy bitching about her stretch marks to notice Robyn ogling her husband. But once Tina had been born, Gloria's whining had grown too much for Robyn to tolerate. Dale was already working off-shore on rigs, probably to get away from Gloria. Hell, Robyn had certainly done all she could to avoid Gloria, and she didn't even live with the woman. If Gloria wasn't complaining about how having a child had ruined her previously perfect body, she was telling the world how beautiful her baby was and how much better than everyone else's child Tina was.

"Gloria was never good enough, never deserved him."

"What was that?"

Robyn jumped with a start. "Dammit, Barbara. Don't sneak up on me. Scared the life out of me. I was just talking to myself."

"I wouldn't worry about it. All the Whites are compassionate. It's just sympathy. Conner's a good looking man. He's not going to settle for a cripple."

"Hmm, you're probably right. But the way he looked at her... I think I'll keep an eye out for him regardless."

After patting her on the shoulder, Barbara moved away from her to clean up the salon, leaving Robyn to her thoughts once again.

She sighed, damn it. Robyn was beginning to wonder if Dale would ever see her like she wanted him to. It was becoming obvious Dale still loved Gloria. Even after she kicked him to the curb to chase their daughter's fame, or when she kicked their daughter to the curb after her injury, he still pined for her. Damn it. How the hell could she win him over? Make him snap out of his delusions. Until she came up with a plan, she needed to keep Tina in her care. Even if having to look at her made her stomach churn. Which meant no men, especially strong handsome firefighters.

Chapter Two

Conner spun around in the darkness. He could sense something—someone—but couldn't see anything in the pitch black. A flash of white caught his eye and he twisted toward it. It flashed again... Hair. Long, straight, white-blond hair. He rubbed his eyes hoping to clear his vision. Another flash had him turning around in the darkness. Green. Emerald green eyes stared at him. So much sorrow in them, Connor's knees buckled under the intensity. As he hit the ground, he saw a glimpse of wheel spokes pass him. Then it returned to peaceful darkness, leaving him alone. The presence that had been was now gone, but Conner couldn't quite catch up with what had happened.

Conner came awake with a jolt. Bolting to sit up in bed, he wiped the sweat off his face. He squeezed his eyes closed as he tried to breathe through the tightness in his chest. With his eyes closed, Conner saw the vision from his dream again. Tina. The young woman he'd seen two weeks ago at the hairdressers before Dominic and Adele's wedding, she was his mate! Little wonder she sent his instincts nuts. Conner's desire to protect her had scared him. As a snow leopard shifter, he was by nature programmed to defend the innocent, but he'd never felt that strong of a protective instinct about anyone—not even Kelly when they went to rescue her and Adele from that sadistic bastard Cole.

Conner swung his legs over the edge of his bed and scrubbed his face in his hands. What should he do now? He'd already gone back to the hairdresser a few times trying to catch her attention, to talk to her and see if he could help her in any way. He wasn't sure what he could do for her, but he'd felt it vital to try to reach the young woman. But that bitch at the salon kept her hidden in the back room, never allowing Conner anywhere near her. He'd not even managed to see Tina since that morning. His mind tripped back to when Dominic started dreaming of Adele. He'd felt pain from Adele as she grieved her mother's death. His dad had explained to them about the mating bond...of course! Dream bonding. Conner could join her in her dreams. His dad had explained that as mates, you could pull the other into your dream or push yourself into theirs. It was how Dominic had first seen his Adele.

Conner eyed the clock showing three in the morning. Great, he could try now. She should be asleep. He rolled back onto his mattress and did as his father had told him and Dominic all those months ago. He focused on Tina, remembering everything he could about her as he drifted back to sleep.

Conner found himself in the stands of a massive gymnasium. Large signs stating 'Olympic Trials' were hung high on the walls and the floor had every setup imaginable on it, from rings to beams, to areas covered in blue mats. He scanned the room for Tina. He couldn't see any wheelchairs, but he would guess she'd dream of being out of it. A loud speaker crackled before calling Tina Anderson up to the uneven bars. Conner made his way down the stands and onto the floor as he watched her approach the bars. She was stunning. All smooth muscle as she gracefully bowed to the judges. Her costume was skin tight, giving Conner a good look at every curve of her body. She was a petite woman, with small breasts and a slight flare out from her waist to her hips. To Conner, she was perfection. The right size for him to wrap up and protect. Her beautiful hair was pulled back into a tight bun, allowing him a good view of her slender sexy neck.

Mesmerized, Connor watched her spin around the bars, every movement exact. Flawless. He saw an expression of panic cross her face as a hand slipped. Out of reflex Conner raced to her, using his supernatural speed to get there in time. As her second hand slipped free, Conner used every ounce of his strength to kick out a side of the lower bar, causing it to crash out of the way. Moments later he held Tina safely in his arms. Even in a muted dream, his whole body shuddered as it came into contact with hers. She gasped as she gripped him tightly around the neck, pressing her hot, sweaty body against his.

People around them were going crazy. He moved off

the mat with Tina. He listened as people ran around with stretchers and gathered near where, had he not caught her, Tina would have been.

"What happened? When I wasn't here."

"I fall. Crash into the lower bar, shattering my femur and cracking my pelvis. It's why I'm stuck in a chair now. This is my real life nightmare. It never goes away. I relive it while I sleep, and suffer the aftereffects while I'm awake."

Unsure what to say, Conner simply held her closer to him, lowering his head to nuzzle against the top of hers.

"Funny that I'm now dreaming of you rescuing me."

"Why is it funny?"

"Because, I only saw you that once. Well, I've seen glimpses of you since. When Robyn sent you away those times, I'd peek out around the curtain to watch you. But I only had that one up close encounter with you. Two weeks ago today."

She began stroking his chest through his t-shirt, before the shirt vanished and she began exploring his naked skin. A grin tugged at his lips. Tina was a little hellcat in her dreams.

"Now, here you are. On the night before my birthday, rescuing me. If only you were there when it really happened."

Burying her face into his neck she began to cry, hard enough her whole body shook. Conner had always been a little awkward around emotional women. Normally, he'd do whatever he could to get away from them, but with Tina it was different. He wanted to soothe her, make her feel better.

"I'm here now, and if I could, I'd turn back time to be there when this happened. So I could rescue you for real."

"Oh, how I wish you were real, Conner."

He had to bite his tongue to stop himself from saying too much. He would love to tell her exactly how real he was, but that wouldn't help. Probably quite the opposite.

"How about we get out of here?"

She raised her head from his chest with a watery grin. "I know just the place."

Tina held his gaze as the world around them spun away and returned as something new. Conner looked around to discover they were now near Sydney on Bondi Beach. Tina must have lived near here at some point. She began squirming in his arms, trying to get down. But Conner had a better idea. He looked down at her with a sly grin, taking in her skimpy little green bikini, moments before he sprinted for the crashing waves. He plowed into the surf with Tina squealing in his arms. In the waist deep water he lowered her to her feet and she gripped his neck tightly, until she remembered that her legs would hold her weight in the dream. With a giggle, she let him go and spun around in the water. Conner's heart felt lighter at her laughter. This is how she should be, carefree and loving life. She put her arms out wide and fell back into the water, allowing herself to sink below the surface. She stood back up moments later and while *she cleared the water from her face, Conner prowled toward her. She was so gorgeous with the sun shining off the droplets of moisture on her skin. She opened her eyes and watched him as he reached for her. Pulling her into his embrace, he crushed his lips against hers. Her taste washed over his senses, tangy citrus with a salty edge from the ocean. He groaned into her mouth as he deepened the kiss, stroking her tongue with his. He felt his body harden and Tina seductively moved her tummy against his hard length.*

"Oh, baby doll, you feel so good. So right in my arms."

"Kiss me again, Conner. Don't ever stop kissing me."

"Now, that's an easy promise to make, and one I intend on never breaking."

And he was sure, once he tasted her in real life, nothing would be able to stop him from keeping his promise.

Jake was pouring himself a coffee when he heard Conner come in to the kitchen.

"Morning. Want a cup?"

"Yeah, morning Dad. Coffee would be great, thanks."

Jake noted Conner's voice was different, a little huskier than usual. He grabbed a second mug down from the cupboard and poured his youngest son a coffee. When he turned to the table to hand it over, he got a good look at his son's face.

"What's wrong, Conner? You're looking like

someone ran over your tail."

Conner's eyes flicked up to him and he could plainly see desperation in them.

"I had a couple of dreams last night...of my mate." Conner paused long enough to take a large mouthful of his coffee, which was testing Jake's nerves. "I know who she is. I've already met her."

Okay, that was great news. Something he would expect Conner to be excited about, not stressed over.

"I would have thought that was a good thing, son. Not many shifters can tell from their first dream."

"I know, Dad. I am excited. But I'm also worried. I met her on the morning of Dom and Adele's wedding. She was at the hairdressers. Robyn, the owner, treated her like shit and wheeled her away from me. She looked miserable. I felt an instant need to protect her. I've been back a couple of times to try and see her, ask her if I can help her in any way, but Robyn keeps her hidden. How am I meant to claim a mate I can't get anywhere near?"

Jake leaned back in his chair and rubbed his chin as he thought about it.

"Do you know her name? Maybe I can use some contacts to find out some information on her."

"Yeah, Tina Anderson. She's in a wheelchair and used to be a gymnast."

"Oh, of course! I remember your mother telling me about her after the wedding. She thought you'd shown a little more interest than usual." He chuckled. "She's going to be harping on about being right for months, you know? How do you know about the gymnast thing?"

"After I woke from the first dream, I instantly knew it was her. I had to see her, so I tried the dream bonding thing you told Dom and me about a while back." Jake listened with interest as his son relayed the dream he'd shared with Tina. "So, don't suppose you or Mum know anything else about her?"

"Not much I'm afraid. Her dad's name is Dale. I went to school with him. He married straight after final year to a real pretty, popular girl. Gloria, I think her name was. Haven't spoken to him in years, but we used to be fairly friendly at school. I'll ask around for you and see what I can dig up for you okay?"

"Thanks, Dad. That'd be great."

Jake noted that Conner's face had lost some of its sadness, the underlying excitement now showing through. He smiled at his youngest son. Watching Conner win over Tina was going to be as much fun as watching Dominic woo Adele last year, he just knew it.

"Do you think Kelly would like to come shopping with me this morning?"

The change in topic grabbed Jake's attention.

"I don't see why not. But what on earth for?"

"It's Tina's twenty-first birthday today. I thought Kelly could help me pick something out for her, and maybe help me sneak it into her at the salon or something."

"I'm sure she'd love to help you shop, Conner. But she'll have no part of you sneaking around."

Jake grinned as Conner's eyes widened in shock at his mother's voice.

"Ah, hi Mum. Sneak up on me next time, why don't you? Just about gave me heart failure. Maybe Kit can join us too. Help Kelly feel more relaxed and all."

Jake couldn't stop the laugh from escaping, "Well, son, if anyone can sneak that present in to Tina, it's Kit."

Kit shook her head as she strolled into the jewelry shop ahead of Conner, but behind Kelly. She was a snow leopard shape shifter, a firefighter, a practical woman who was strong and independent. She was not a girly-girl, certainly wasn't into shopping for anything other than necessities. Yet here she was, for the second time in so many months, helping one of the White boys buy jewelry for his mate. Mind you, she had enjoyed helping Dominic pick out Adele's engagement ring. At twenty-eight she was starting to wonder if her mate would ever show up. Kit hated that the males got to dream of their mates, but the females had to just sit back and hope her mate would get off his ass and come look for her.

Kelly's small hand slipped into hers, which pulled her from her introspection. Kit looked down at Kelly and smiled. Such a sweet kid. It didn't seem that long ago when Kit had carried the catatonic girl out of Cole's basement. Now she was a vibrant pre-teen, still painfully shy, but once she got to know you, she was a real spitfire of a girl.

"So, Kelly, what do you think Conner should give his lady love?"

"Something pretty."

Kit couldn't help but chuckle at the cute way Kelly screwed up her nose in thought.

"Silver. Silver will look nice with her hair."

"I agree, silver it is. How about a necklace?"

"I didn't realize you'd noticed her, Kelly."

Conner's voice brought Kelly's head around to focus on him.

"Of course I noticed her, Uncle Conner. When that mean lady screeched at her, she looked up and I saw her eyes. They looked really sad, like mine did before." Kelly paused a moment, "She's not happy, she's suffering where she is. You *have* to help her, Uncle Conner."

She'd started shaking as she spoke and Kit gathered her in close.

"It's okay, Kelly. You're safe. Cole's gone. We got you."

"But what about her? The sad lady at the salon? Who's got her?"

Conner came in close and stroked Kelly's curls behind her ear, "I've got Tina, honey. I just have to work out a way to get around that mean lady to get to her. But once I do, I'll always protect her. Now, how about we have a look at some of these pretty necklaces?"

Kit felt Kelly tighten her arms around her waist briefly before she released her and stepped toward the glass cabinets filled with necklaces and other jewelry. Kit tried to push away the oily feeling in her chest that she was picking something special, a physical sign of Conner's affection for someone else, when no one had ever gone to this effort for her.

"Oh, oh, oh! I found it, Uncle Conner! Kit, come look. It's perfect."

Kit allowed Kelly's joy to rub off on her. The kid was so excited. She looked through the glass to the pendant Kelly was pointing at. It was perfect. Before they left to come shopping, Conner had confessed the dream he'd shared with Tina about Bondi Beach and his vow to never stop kissing her. The cute little necklace Kelly found was a silver heart, outlined with diamond chips inlaid around the top right corner and the lower left edge. What made it perfect was the yellow gold paw print on the lower right edge.

"Don't think you'll get any more perfect than that. The diamonds are forever, the paw print is you and, well, the heart is pretty self-explanatory."

Conner nodded in agreement with her. "Wow. Well done, Kelly. What a find! It's definitely the perfect choice. Let me go get the sales assistant and we'll be done here."

As Conner wandered away, Kelly pulled her down to whisper to her.

"Can we keep shopping?"

"Sure, kiddo. What did you want to buy?"

"I really like your shoes."

Kit let loose a loud laugh. "They are pretty cool. Okay, shoe shop is the next stop."

Her cherry red Doc Martins had always been her favorite and had often drawn attention. They were a little pricey, but she'd spend the money without a problem to see Kelly smile like she was right now.

Half an hour later Kit sat chatting to Conner while Kelly tried on every pair of Doc Martin boots the store had in her size.

"So, how are you planning on getting that present to Tina?"

Conner's mega-watt smile gave away his intentions. She sighed. "You want me to deliver it?"

"Well, I was hoping you'd be able to slip it to her at the salon. Robyn won't let me near the place. How else can I do it?"

"You want me to tell her who it's from? Or are you going for the secret admirer angle?"

"I was going to give you a letter to go with it. Thinking I'd go around to her house tonight. Maybe if I hang around till after Robyn turns in for the night, Tina can come out to meet me."

"Better tell her who you are then. No way will a woman in a wheelchair agree to meet a complete stranger late at night."

Conner rubbed the back of his neck. "Yeah, you better ask her for her address too then. I mean, I know where she lives, but I don't want her to think I'm some weird stalker."

Kit laughed. "Nah, you're not a weird stalker at all, more of a friendly lovable one."

Conner lightly thumped her arm as he shook his head at her.

"I found them! My favorite ones. I'm going to wear them all the time just like you do."

Kelly's excited voice drew both their attention, and Conner fussed over the black boots with small purple flowers printed over the leather while Kit headed to the counter to pay for them.

Tina re-read the letter for the hundredth time. The only thing she'd received to mark this day as different from any other was this short note and a pair of emerald earrings from her father. She fingered the gem in her ear. Her father loved her and missed her like crazy. His letter was filled with promises of this being his last long trip working overseas. He was missing his sweet pea too much to do it again. She wiped tears from her eyes as she smiled and folded the letter up and tucked it back into the side pocket of her cargo pants.

"Happy twenty-first birthday," she quietly said to herself. Even if she did have to wait for it, her father coming home for good was the best present she could ever get. No more Robyn. Tina looked at the Windows logo pinging around the screen saver on the computer. It was her damn birthday. She didn't want to work today, especially since she didn't even get paid for it. She glanced through the curtain to see both Barbara and

Robyn working with clients.

Perfect.

Tugging her gloves into place, she headed to the back door and wheeled herself outside. She knew she'd cop hell from Robyn for leaving but she didn't care. It was her day and she'd do whatever she wanted. And she wanted to breathe in the fresh air, to be away from the chemicals of the salon's back room.

"Hey, Tina! Have you got a minute?"

Tina twisted to look behind her up the footpath. A tall—gorgeous—red haired woman was jogging toward her.

"Do I know you?"

The woman rubbed the back of her neck. "Not yet. My name is Kit. I work at the fire station. I'm good friends with the White boys. With Conner."

Tina spun her chair around so she was facing the woman.

"You're friends with Conner? So why are you here?"

"Conner's been trying to get to you. He wants to see you, but Robyn won't let him get near you. So..." she paused to hand over a small wrapped package and an envelope, "he asked me to deliver your birthday present from him, along with the letter. Happy twenty-first, Tina."

Tears formed unbidden in her eyes. This stranger was being so nice, and had given her the only in-person 'happy birthday' she'd received all day.

"Thank you. But I still don't understand."

"You will. Read the letter, and give Conner a chance. He's a good man, Tina. He'll never do you wrong."

With a gentle smile, Kit turned and strolled away, leaving Tina frozen in shock, holding her gift and letter. Snapping out of it, she rested the items in her lap before she wheeled herself down the street to the small park where she could sit in the sun and relax.

Applying her chair's brake, she opened the box. She never could resist opening the present first. The cards were always read second at her birthday parties. Her mother had hated the habit, saying it was rude and how important it was to make sure you knew who gave you what. She'd never forgotten who gave her presents, didn't matter which order she opened things.

The breath froze in her lungs as she flipped open the jewelers box. A beautiful silver and diamond heart, with a sweet little paw print. She quickly took it from the box and clasped it behind her neck. The chain hung snuggly to her so the pendant sat in the hollow at the base of her throat. The smooth metal felt good against her skin. She packed the box away and opened the envelope. A single piece of crisp white paper slipped free, the writing done by hand. So much more personal and special than computer print. She settled back in her chair to read Conner's note.

Tina,

I hope you like your present. I wish I could have given it to you in person, but I can't get near you. If *you want, text me your address. I'll come over late tonight, after she goes to bed. We can just sit out in your backyard and chat.*

Happy 21st Birthday, baby.

XO

Conner

She traced her fingers over the black inked letters, large broad masculine strokes made up the words. His phone number was written under his name. Ten numbers that she somehow knew would irrevocably change her life if she chose to use them and turn to him. But would it be for the better? Thinking about how Robyn treated her, it couldn't possibly be worse.

Squaring her shoulders and taking a deep breath, she pulled her phone out and sent the most important text she'd ever written.

Luv my present. ThankU. 36 Pitt Dr. After 11pm. Txt me wen u get here.

Moments later, her phone beeped that a new message had come in.

I'm glad. Can't w8 4 2nite. C U @ 11

With her heart in her throat, she wheeled back to the salon. She hadn't been this happy or excited since before her accident. Her dream from the previous night floated through her mind. Conner spinning her through the waves at Bondi.

She made it back to the salon and peeked through the curtain, happy to see her absence hadn't been noticed.

She went back to the computer and spent the afternoon working, all the while dreaming about one very sexy firefighter, Conner White.

Chapter Three

Conner's heart raced as he pulled up outside Tina's house. Grabbing his phone, he shot off a text.

I'm here.

He was meeting his mate. Albeit creeping around in the dark like teenagers, but still. He was going to be able to touch her in the flesh. Quietly exiting his car, he wiped his sweaty palms down his jeans. He silently jogged around to the back of the house, easily vaulting over the fence. He made his way over to a swing that hung from a big tree in the rear of the yard and sat. He didn't have to wait long before his beautiful mate came out the rear door, rolling silently down the ramp at the back of the house. He stayed still, allowing her to come to him.

Conner didn't want to frighten Tina, and she looked very nervous. A shaft of moonlight glinted off her necklace. She was wearing his gift. It melted his heart that she honestly liked it enough to put it straight on. He spread his legs to give her more room as she wheeled in close to his front. Unfortunately, she stopped before she was that close.

"Hey."

"Hey, yourself. Glad you like the pendant."

He leaned forward to brush his finger around the heart design, grazing her skin lightly with the tip. Sparks shot up his arm at the light contact and he watched as Tina's eyes slid shut on a gasp. He let his hand drop away, gripping the swing ropes to prevent himself from wrapping her up in his embrace. He toed the ground and moved the seat a little. Tina watched the movement with longing.

"I haven't swung on that since I was a kid."

"Would you like to? I can help you; keep you safe while you swing."

She went to shake her head but stopped as Conner rose and moved toward her. He couldn't believe his good fortune. He was hoping tonight might end in a small kiss, but to hold her in his arms, even if for only a moment was too good to be true.

Slipping his arm beneath her knees, he scooped her out of her chair and against his chest. His heart leapt at the contact. Her citrus scent teased his senses as he filled his lungs with air. As he smoothly made his way over to the swing with her, she relaxed against him, resting her head on his chest. It felt so right. He gently lowered her to sit on the swing and she wrapped her hands tightly around the ropes. Looking down at her feet the way she was prevented Conner from seeing her face, so he smoothly dropped to his knees beside her.

"Tina? Are you okay? I didn't hurt you did I?"

She shook her head and tightened her grip on the

ropes, so much so, that he could see her knuckles turning white. With a finger beneath her chin, he tilted her face up. With gentleness he wiped away her tears. His mind whirled. What had he done to upset her? How could he fix it? Make her smile.

"Don't cry, Tina. Please, I can't take you being sad. Want me to put you back in your chair?"

She rolled her lips in before releasing them and taking a shaky breath. "Would you...um, hold me? Please."

Would he hold her? It took him less than a heartbeat to have her back in his arms. He settled himself on the swing and rocked back and forth with her as he kissed the top of her head.

"I'm sorry. I'm such a mess." She lifted her head from his chest and pressed her hand over his heart. "If you want to leave, I understand."

Was the woman mad? He would never leave her, but he knew it was too soon to be making such declarations.

"I don't want to leave, Tina. I like spending time with you, holding you like this."

His heart swelled as the moonlight showed him the blush that rose over her cheeks and the small smile that played at the edges of her lips.

"You must be crazy. Who'd want to spend time with an overly emotional cripple?"

Conner hissed in a breath, her insult to herself cutting through him like a knife.

"You are beautiful, Tina. You are most certainly not a cripple. Who would tell you such a thing?"

"Robyn and Barbara at the salon. They say it about me—or to me—regularly."

He was infuriated for her that she had to live with such abuse. He'd also begun to question what else the women did to Tina, aside from verbal insults.

"Oh, Tina, baby. That's on them, not you. Their insults only show how insecure and childish they are. It's not anything to do with who you are."

With a slight shake of her head, Tina changed the topic of conversation. "You haven't asked how I got in the chair. It's normally the first thing people ask."

"What put you in the chair is in the past. I'm much more concerned with you now. And I know you'll tell me when you're ready. I'm in no rush."

"But the past makes us who we are now. You can't possibly know me now without knowing what happened."

Conner understood she wanted to talk about her accident. To be honest, if she told him, it would make life easier as he wouldn't have to pretend he didn't know anymore.

"You can tell me about it anytime you want. I'm not going to pressure you about it."

She began playing with a button on his shirt, tickling the flesh beneath as she told him about the accident he'd already seen in their dream.

"So, you'll be out of the chair one day?"

"Hmm, with rehab maybe. But I'm not getting it. Robyn is supposed to do the exercises with me, but she doesn't lift a finger. She thinks I don't see what she's about, but I see her clear as day."

"What do you mean? Why wouldn't she help you with your rehab?"

"Robyn likes my dad. My mother stole him out from under her in high school. From what I understand, dad has never really noticed Robyn. He's always been all about mum. Crazy man. Anyway, I'm pretty sure Robyn took on being my caretaker to get in good with my dad. She knows if I get better that's all over."

His grip tightened on her. *That bitch*! Tina's light caress over his clenched jaw drew his attention from his fury, "I can only guess that is why she's keeping you away too. I mean, if I had a boyfriend who was willing to help me, she wouldn't be needed."

His whole body was tense with rage and frustration. He wanted to tell her he was willing—more than willing—to care for her. To keep her safe forever with him, but Conner knew he couldn't talk like that yet. He'd scare her.

"Why don't you leave? I mean, she's not helping you recover. Wouldn't you be better off on your own?"

Her gaze dropped away from him, and she twisted her hands together in her lap. Damn, he shouldn't have voiced the questions. But they'd slipped from his mouth before he'd really thought them through.

"Where would I go? How would I get a place to live? What would I do? I have no money, no skills that would help me gain employment."

"I could—"

She cut him off by pressing two fingers against his lips, "We've only just met, Conner. I don't know you well enough to run away with you. No matter how much I'm tempted."

Needing to release at least some of the emotions running around his mind, he kissed her fingers before gently peeling them away from his mouth. He palmed her face, tilted it up to his and lowered his lips to hers. He sipped at her lips. Light tender kisses to convey his deep feelings for her. Her fingers gripped his head as she deepened the kiss with a small moan. He was lost to the taste of her, tangy citrus filling his senses. Her tongue stroked against his, and Conner groaned as he hardened further against her soft bottom. She was driving him insane with lust. He pulled back from her mouth, panting. With closed eyes, he rested his forehead against hers. Her finger, cool from the night air, traced his lips.

"You are an amazing kisser."

"Really? Because I've never done it before."

The words left his mouth before his desire soaked brain could stop them. He silently cursed as her body stiffened.

"You can't expect me to believe a guy that looks as good as you has never kissed a girl before."

"Looks aren't everything, baby doll. And I've never wanted to kiss anyone before you, so I haven't."

"Well, you can kiss me any time you like."

"Hmmm, is that so?" He pressed his mouth against

hers again to have another taste. He would never get enough of her. She pulled back this time, stroking his face as she did.

"I'd best be getting back inside before Robyn figures out what we're up to."

"Can I come back tomorrow night? I'll wait back here for you. I promise she won't see me or my car."

"That sounds divine. Thank you, Conner."

"It's my pleasure, Tina."

He reluctantly rose from the swing and settled her in her chair before he wheeled her over to the ramp. He bent and kissed her neck before whispering in her ear, "Happy birthday, baby doll. Sweet dreams." He rose and strode away, jumping the fence and jogging back to his car, all the while trying to work out a way to get Tina away from Robyn's care.

In a daze, Tina made her way to her room. Glancing out the window, she was just in time to see Conner's car quietly roll down the street. With fingers brushing her lips, she smiled. Sparks of happiness zinged through her body as she stripped and hauled herself into bed. Usually she'd be in tears of frustration, after struggling to get through her nightly routine. Not tonight. Tonight she was giddy with excitement.

Conner White was as beautiful in real life as he'd been in her dream. She hoped she would dream of him again tonight. She frowned, knowing she would have to keep him hidden from Robyn. Tina didn't want to think about what the crazy bitch would do if she found out about their little late night get-together. Her worry washed away as she thought about the fact he'd be waiting for her again tomorrow night.

Conner couldn't have known what it had meant to be able to sit on her swing. Memories of her as a small child filled her mind, her daddy pushing her higher as she squealed in delight. Back before her training had taken up all her time. Before her mother took over her life. The more time she had to reflect on her childhood and career, the more she resented her mother. With little to no consideration for Tina, she had pushed and forced her so hard. Even when she won awards and accolades—it was never enough. Perfection was her mother's requirement of her, at all times, in all things. Her father was different though. His love was unconditional and simple. Pure, as a parent's love should be.

In their bonding time after her accident, he'd told her how sorry he was that he hadn't fought for her. He'd thought she was happy with her gymnastics, so he went along with Gloria's plans. She'd seen the pain in his eyes. Tina had tried to tell him it wasn't his fault, but he wouldn't hear it. She half believed her dad had taken the long job away in an attempt to escape his misguided guilt regarding her. She sighed. When he found out how Robyn had been treating her, he'd feel even worse. But she couldn't tell him. Especially now he'd told her this was the last time he'd leave her for so long. She wouldn't jeopardize his returning to her simply so she could vent her frustrations. Besides, she had Conner to focus on now. He'd allow her to keep a bubble around her mind. So long as she thought about Conner, Robyn's shit couldn't penetrate into her psyche to take effect.

Rolling over and curling up, she nuzzled into her pillow, wishing it were Conner's chest, as she allowed herself to drift off to sleep.

Curling her toes into the sand, she grinned. The feeling of freedom to be able to move without limitation was the best sensation. Taking off, she sprinted across the sand. She executed a perfect cartwheel followed by a somersault, laughing with pure joy as she finished with a pirouette. Strong arms wrapped around her, pulling her back to a hard chest. She took a deep breath and absorbed Conner's scent. Cedarwood and sage. The smell made her feel cocooned in warmth, like the humidity of a rainforest—without the suffocating effect, of course.

"I love to hear you laugh, baby doll."

"Hmmm, Conner. You smell so good. Better in real life, but still."

His deep chuckle in her ear brought out goose bumps on her flesh.

"You smell pretty good yourself. All citrusy fresh and entirely irresistible."

He nibbled down her neck, caressing her flat stomach with his large masculine hands. She reached a hand up and tousled his hair. The thick strands felt so good against her fingers. He gripped her hips and turned her to face him, taking her mouth with his as soon as he could.

Oh, how I wish this was real.

Breathless, she pulled from the kiss. She stroked his face with her fingertips, caressing and memorizing each inch of his beauty. The realization that this was just a dream brought tears to her eyes.

"This can never be my reality...and it sucks that my dreams would tease me like this."

She whirled around and sprinted from him, from the pain threatening to envelope her. She made it to the lifeguard tower and slumped to her knees beneath its shelter, sobbing and panting. She was such a fool to torment herself with such fantasies. Suddenly, she was scooped up and held against a firm chest.

"Oh, baby, it'll be real. Just you wait. This will be our reality, one day. I will find a way to get past Robyn, to get you free of her."

"You have no idea how much I want this dream to be real, Conner. I can't stand my life! I'm locked away, forced to work in that tiny back room of the salon, not allowed out or to speak to anyone. She's turned me into a ghost! The only spark of life I've had was Kit slipping me your present and note, then meeting you at my swing."

"Oh, Tina...I will find a way. I promise I'll make it better. Just hang in there for me, please."

Wrapped in Conner's strong embrace, she allowed herself to lean on him. Why the hell couldn't this be real? Surely after all she'd suffered this last year, she deserved something good, some happiness? And Conner would make a wonderful knight in shining armor.

Chapter Four

Robyn tapped a perfectly manicured nail against her lips as she watched Tina. Something was different about her. She couldn't quite place it. She looked a little different, her shoulders straighter, her face not quite so pathetically sad all the time. In fact, a ghost of a smile graced her lips. As Tina wheeled back from the coffee table, the lounge light reflected on something around her throat.

"What are you wearing around your neck, Tina? Where did it come from?"

"It's just a necklace, Robyn. Nothing special."

Robyn frowned, the clench of Tina's jaw said otherwise.

"I don't believe you. Who gave you the necklace?"

Tina turned to her, anger written clearly over her features. This was not good. Tina never showed any emotion, other than crying all the damn time.

"It is none of your business who gave it to me."

"Like hell it is!"

She flew to her feet as Tina raced to her room. Before Tina could slam the door, Robyn was there, pushing her way in. There was only one person who could have this effect on Tina. How had he gotten past her? She'd been so careful to never let Tina out of her sight since Conner had shown his interest.

"It's from that boy, Conner, isn't it? How did he get to you?"

Tina backed toward her window with fear in her gaze. She should fear her. Robyn was in one hell of a mood. A phone chime caught her attention.

"Give me your phone."

Why hadn't she taken it off her earlier? Tina didn't need a damn phone. Gloria mentally shook her head, such a dumb mistake for her to make.

"No. You can't do this to me! I'm an adult. I have rights."

She laughed with zero humor. "No, honey, you don't. You're nothing but a cripple. No one will believe your stories and your father made me your primary caregiver. He was even so kind as to sign legal documentation to that effect. So, I can do whatever I want with you. Give. Me. Your. Phone."

Tina tried to keep hold of her phone but her hands were trembling and Robyn swiftly snatched it free from her grasp. Robyn quickly activated the screen and went into the messages. Her fury grew at each one she read. Tina had been sneaking out at night to meet Conner for the past two weeks! Body vibrating with rage, she turned the phone off and pocketed it. She prowled over to Tina, who was as close to the window as she could get.

"You will *never* see Conner again. Are we clear?"

As Tina nodded jerkily, Robyn reached forward and ripped the necklace from around her neck. Opening the window with a jerk, she tossed it though, before slamming it closed and turning the lock in place. She turned back to see Tina rubbing at the red line around her neck. Served herself right, she should have known better than to attempt to take up with a boy.

"Now let's get you tucked into bed for the night, shall we?"

She helped Tina into bed then left the room—with her chair. After parking it in the walk-in-closet in her bedroom, she made certain both the back and front doors were dead-bolted. No way was that boy entering her house. She turned toward her room and shook her head at the sound of Tina's sobbing. *Stupid girl.*

She made her way back to the closet and brushed her hand over Dale's clothes to stir up his scent. Dale didn't wear cologne. His smell was pure masculinity. She was supposed to be staying in the spare room down the hall, but she loved being surrounded by Dale's things, his scent. She slept in his bed, on his sheets. Every night she dreamt of him joining her in that bed. One day. One day he would notice her and fall at her feet. Then she wouldn't have to put up with Tina at all, but send her away to some rehab facility until she could fend for herself.

Conner parked around the corner in his usual spot before heading to Tina's house. As he got close he could sense something was wrong. Instead of going straight around the back, he crept over the lawn to crouch below her window. He could hear her sobbing, the sound ripping into his heart. He lowered himself on all fours on the ground, sinking his fingers into the grass, trying desperately not to shift. His leopard wanted to protect and comfort his mate. So did his human side, but he couldn't, as he had no way of entering her room without alerting Robyn.

Something cold against his palm caused him to start. Raising his hand he saw Tina's necklace lying against the grass, the one she hadn't taken off since he gave it to her two weeks ago. His instincts flared, putting his body and mind on high alert. There was no way Tina would throw it away. He held it closer to his face to inspect the chain. Sure enough, it was broken. A growl formed low in his throat. Had Robyn discovered their secret nighttime rendezvous?

He sprinted back to his car, using every bit of willpower he had to not shift and go back to take her away. Once inside the confines of his vehicle, he rang Tina's number. Straight to voicemail, meaning it was turned off. Shit, Robyn must have found out. Barely aware of his actions, he started his car and headed home. Dream bonding was the only way he could see her now. But that would never be enough for either of them. He had to figure out how to get her away from Robyn. Quickly.

As he plowed through the front door he nearly took

out his dad, who was walking through to the lounge room.

"Sorry, Dad."

"No worries, son. You're not looking so hot there. What happened? Is Tina okay?"

"I don't know if she's okay. We've been meeting up at night in her backyard. I think Robyn's found out. I found her necklace outside her window. I could hear her sobbing and her phone is turned off."

His dad's face grew serious as he gripped Conner's shoulder. "Robyn is not a nice person. I've been asking around, trying to get information about Tina for you. No one who knows Robyn wants to be on her bad side. She's got a real mean streak. Dale mustn't know about what's going on. No way would he allow this kind of treatment to happen to his little girl. I'll see if I can find out what rig he's on. See if I can ring or email him. Let him know he needs to come home. You going to dream bond with her tonight?"

"That's what I was planning to do. It's the only way I've got to communicate with her now. I'm thinking I might try to tell her the dreams are real. Not sure. The last dream we shared she lost the plot. Broke down in tears before getting angry with herself for dreaming up something she'll never have. Dad, she desperately wanted the dream to be real but she wouldn't believe me when I told her that one day it would be. She sounded depressed and close to doing something really dangerous. Scared the hell out of me, Dad."

"Well, you better get to bed then, son. I'll do what I can to contact her father. We will fix this, and get her out safely."

"I know Dad. I just wish I could think how! Maybe if I was an alpha, I would have figured something out already…" He finished off quietly, more to himself, but his dad still heard him.

His dad gave him a small shake before he gripped his face between his hands, forcing Conner to look into his gaze. "Don't you ever think for one moment that you are less of a man, because you're not the alpha, or future alpha. We are all simply men, and we make mistakes. Do you think Dominic doesn't kick himself daily for not checking the house before he let Kelly go back to her room? Or that he didn't go with Adele when she went to check on her? In hindsight, he can see he was more focused on stopping a future incident when he should have been paying more attention to what was under his nose. Leaving the girls in the house while he went outside to make that phone call resulted in Cole getting his filthy hands on both of them. He hurt Adele and Kelly because of Dominic's poor choice. He'll always feel guilty about it, but in the end, as a leap, as a family, we got the girls out and safe. The same applies here. We will all pull together and help you get Tina out safely."

Pulling free of his father's grip, Conner looked to the floor. He could feel heat rising in his cheeks as embarrassment from his childish words set in. He'd always felt inferior to Dominic, he wasn't sure why. His parents and his brother never did anything to make him feel less, but he did. As the second son of the current alpha he was overlooked publicly. With no real role in the leap, he often felt like a spare wheel. He kept it hidden most of the time, not allowing the feelings to surface, but every so often they would break through his control.

He could sense his mother coming closer and he just couldn't handle what she would say to him. He was already on edge with worry about Tina. Without further thought, he turned and bolted up the hallway to the other end of the house where his bedroom was located. In his room, Conner quickly worked his way through his nightly routine. Once under the covers, he forced his body to relax and his mind to clear of all thoughts except those of Tina, hoping she was already asleep.

He found himself in a dense rainforest, dark and damp. The depressed tone of the place weighed down on him heavily. He began searching for Tina. She had to be here. Hearing a faint sob, he headed towards the sound. He found a waterfall and looked up.

His breath caught in his throat. There she was, standing at the top of the waterfall, on a large smooth rock protruding out of the flow. Her back was turned toward the drop, and her body shook as she cried. He watched her stretch her arms out wide and step back closer to the edge. Panic overtook him as realization dawned; she was trying to kill herself! Even in a dream where he knew she couldn't truly die, the thought tore at him. He roared as he shifted and bounded up the side of the fall to get to her.

She'd stopped and turned at his roar. She now stood frozen in place as he came closer. He strode through the water easily and wound his feline body around her legs, forcing her further from the drop. He continued to herd her toward the safety of the bank as he tried to calm his racing heart. Once she was safely out of the water, he moved away and shifted to human. Thankfully, being a dream, he could also materialize some clothes. He didn't want his nudity to distract either of them.

"What the hell, Tina? You can't do that! Not even in a dream. I need you. I can't live in a world where you don't exist! I'm trying to find a way to get you away from Robyn. Dad's helping me. It shouldn't take us long. But I need you to hold on for me."

"You- You were a cat. A really big cat."

He dropped down to his knees in front of her. "There are things I need to tell you, baby doll. The fact I'm a snow leopard shifter is one of them. The other is about these dreams of ours. We're both here. I'm not a figment of your imagination. I am me."

She shook her head slightly, then began talking as if he hadn't spoken, hadn't shifted from animal to man, "I can't do this. I hurt, I hurt so much. I just want it to stop." Her gaze went to the waterfall, filled with longing.

He tilted her face away from the drop and toward his. "It will stop. I'll get you free of Robyn. Then you and I can start the rest of our lives. Can you trust me to fix *this?"*

She cupped his face in her soft palms. "How can I know you are really here? That my subconscious isn't trying to throw you at me as a last ditch effort to prevent what I want to do."

"Ask me something. Something you don't know about me."

"What year were you born?"

"1988, tenth of September."

Taking her hands from his face, she began to rub her temple, like she was getting a headache. "This really is too much, Conner. Okay, assuming that is your birthday, you're really here with me. What about the snow leopard thing? Is that real or just here in our dream?"

Conner couldn't bear not having her in his arms another moment. He scooped her up and sat down with her nestled in his lap. Just like a kitten, she curled into him, seeking comfort.

"It's real. There are quite a few shifters in Rosebery. Pretty much the entire fire crew and their families for a start."

She was shaking her head, no doubt having trouble assimilating this new information.

To give her a break, he changed the subject. "Want to tell me what happened tonight? I found your necklace outside your window. The chain is broken."

Tina's hand went to her throat and Conner growled low as his anger grew. She had a thin red line around the back and side of her neck.

"Robyn tore it off me. She went crazy. Well, more crazy than usual. Took my phone, told me I couldn't see you ever again. She helped me into bed then took my chair with her when she left. I can't get anywhere without it. I have so little movement in my pelvis, and my bones are still healing. There's no way my leg would hold my weight. Even if it did, I'm not strong enough to fight her. She has one hundred percent control over me and I hate it. I hate it so much, Conner."

With a sob she clung to him, burying her face in his neck. He stroked her back in soothing circles. His chest tight with emotion, he lowered his head to her. Kissing his way down her neck—paying special attention to the red line—before moving over her shoulder. Her tears slowed and he felt her nuzzle against his skin, unknowingly marking herself with his scent. His leopard purred with satisfaction, even as his heart continued to break for her pain. She tilted away from him, opening the long line of her throat to him. He accepted the invitation and left feather light kisses in his wake as he made his way up to her lips.

Cradling her face in his palms, he devoured her mouth, slipping his tongue in to dance with hers. She moaned and shuddered beneath him. He felt her soft caress as she slipped the buttons free on his shirt. He laid her down on the soft mossy grass and sat up, stripping his shirt before covering her body with his and diving back between her lips. He pulled back with a hiss as she tilted her pelvis against his rock hard erection. Moving to her side he slid his hand up her body, caressing her from hip to ribs. Slipping under her shirt, he traced her ribs up to her breasts. He stopped in shock as he came in contact with flesh, not material.

"No bra, baby?"

"I'm small enough that I don't need to always wear one."

He watched, frozen, as she peeled her shirt up and off, revealing her perfect breasts. He couldn't look away. She was stunning. Purring, he lowered his head to her, nuzzling his face in her cleavage before rising up to suckle a beaded nipple into his mouth. She arched into him, gripping his hair in her fists as he lavished attention on her flesh. Never had he tasted anything so delicious. How much better would it be in real life? He couldn't wait to find out.

Her hands played over his shoulders and upper back before sliding down his arms. He occupied his fingers by caressing every square inch of her he could reach. He gripped the fly of her pants and she pulled his head up from her skin.

"Not here, not in a dream. I need to feel you in the real world, I need to be one hundred percent sure it's real."

He kissed her with all the love he was feeling for this wonderful woman.

"Sounds good to me. I can't wait." He snuggled against her on the mossy forest floor, enjoying simply holding her in his embrace where he could keep her safe.

"C'mon Dominic, we need to get going."

Adele gave her husband a small shove toward the door. They had been away for a month on an extended honeymoon. After all the drama of Cole kidnapping Kelly and Adele, then Adele shifting for the first time, Dominic insisted they take a full month to holiday, relax and recover. Having Dominic all to herself twenty-four/seven had been amazing. She smiled as she remembered their visit to see the original shifter, Choden Sangye, high in the Tibetan mountains. She'd loved being able to shift and run as a leopard in the dense forest, to feel the cold of the snow on the pads of her feet. She shivered as remembered excitement raced through her. The feel of fur against fur when Dominic would nuzzle against her had made her heart melt and her body heat. But, as wonderful as it had all been, she'd missed Kelly something fierce and couldn't wait to get back to her foster daughter.

"Kelly won't even be out of bed yet, beautiful. What's the rush?"

"Please Dominic. I need to see her."

He leaned in to kiss her, before he whispered against her lips. "Why didn't we collect her yesterday then?"

With a nervous smile, she responded. "I had something I had to do before we picked her up."

Dominic raised an eyebrow at her in question, but she wasn't telling him. At least not yet.

"All will be revealed very soon, *mon amour*, I

promise."

While away, she'd had an idea. So far, she'd kept it to herself, not wanting to get everyone's hopes up. Well, she had discussed it with Choden. Adele had great respect for the Tibetan Buddhist culture, but she didn't know much about it. So she had asked Choden if he would help her. Of course the gentle monk had readily agreed, thinking her idea wonderful.

Then soon after they had touched down yesterday, she'd received a phone call from Detective Alex Ross. Using DNA they had identified the remains of Kelly's mother. Her body had been found washed up on the beach further down the coast from Strahan about eight months ago. After thirty days her body had remained unclaimed, so following protocol, she had been buried at the Strahan cemetery in an unmarked grave.

That information had changed her plans. She'd originally wanted to hold a memorial at the remains of Cole's house, but now she'd have it at the grave site. She'd also contacted a funeral home and made plans to have a headstone made for Kelly's mother. The police were still researching her history, learning details. Even simple things like her full name were still unknown. Kelly knew her first name was Lisa, but no more. Her poor little girl couldn't remember ever celebrating her birthday. Such a sad life Kelly had lived. Even before Cole had captured her and her mother, they'd been on the run, living day to day and barely surviving.

Her time spent at the police station had been

beneficial. Constable Ross was very helpful. He'd explained how they were searching for details and paperwork on Kelly and Lisa. Currently, he was preparing the necessary forms for Kelly and Adele to apply to Victims of Crime for a grant. Adele was hoping the grants would cover the cost of the headstone, and the burial costs they owed. Now they needed to wait for the government cogs to turn. But her plans were concrete enough that she could tell everyone about them. She'd resisted telling Dominic—not because she liked secrets. She hated them. Adele was a firm believer they had no place in a relationship but Dominic was simply too adorable when he begged her to tell him about it, for her to resist teasing him a little. A tap on her nose brought her back to reality.

"Where'd you go? You looked very deep in thought there."

"I was, and I'll reveal all at your parents' place. You ready?"

"Yep, sure am. Has this big secret got anything to do with your disappearing act yesterday?"

"Most definitely."

With her sweetest smile in place, she snatched the keys from Dominic's hand and raced out to the car. She didn't make it. She giggled as Dominic swept her off her feet and carried her to the passenger side of the car. She unlocked the car and Dominic awkwardly opened the door without releasing his hold on her. Placing Adele in the seat, he leaned in for a searing kiss, getting her so hot, she barely felt him take the keys from her fingers.

"You just relax, beautiful. I'll drive."

"Yeah, you do that." *Because after a kiss like that, my brain can't function well enough to drive.*

She knew she had a goofy grin on her face, but didn't care in the least as she watched her sexy husband prowl around the bonnet of the Rav4 to the driver's door.

Moments later they were on their way to his parents' house where Kelly had been staying. Adele was filled with a mixture of excitement and nervousness. Both emotions sent the butterflies in her stomach into overdrive. She sincerely hoped she wouldn't be sick.

Dominic eyed his wife warily as they walked up to the house. She had a secret, and she was having way too much fun keeping it from him.

"You can't even give me a hint before you tell everyone?"

"Nope. It's your own fault, *mon cher*. You're just so cute when you're frustrated."

He growled low at his cheeky mate as he reached to grip her hips. The front door swinging open prevented him from doing any more.

For the moment.

Adele was so going to pay for teasing him later.

"Adele!" Kelly's high pitched squeal pierced his eardrums as the young girl sprinted toward them—still wearing her pajamas—throwing herself into Adele's embrace.

He watched with pride as Adele wrapped her in her arms and cuddled her tightly. "Oh, my *ma chère,* I missed you."

"I missed you too. And Dominic. Did you have fun?"

"We had lots of fun. Next holiday we'll take you too, I promise."

As Adele released Kelly, Dominic swooped in to give her a hug and twirl her around before setting her back down. "Missed you too, kiddo. You're definitely coming with us next time."

"Come inside all of you! Kelly's not the only one who missed you, you know."

He looked to the doorway to see his mother standing there, arms crossed with the biggest grin spread over her face. He strode over to her to kiss her cheek and give her a hug. "Hi, Mum. I'd spin you around too, but you'd probably slap me for it."

"Too right I would, my boy."

Patting his cheek, she moved back into the house with them all following her.

Everyone settled in the lounge room. Kelly stole the seat next to Adele, snuggling into her side. Dominic sat in a single chair opposite with a chuckle. His girls were so sweet. His dad came in with a tray of coffees, and a hot chocolate for Kelly. Once everyone had their drinks, Dominic cocked a brow at Adele.

"Well, beautiful, are you going to put me out of my misery now? We're all here."

"You are so easy to tease, Dominic. I've had a secret

for less than a week and you're just about jumping out of your skin." She shook her head at him with a giggle. "Okay, I received a very interesting phone call yesterday..."

Dominic sat awestruck as Adele relayed everything that she'd accomplished yesterday. Part of him felt hurt she hadn't needed his help, but mostly he was extremely proud of her. His wife and mate was an extraordinary female indeed.

"Someone found her. So she's really dead." Kelly's whisper cut through the room like a sharp knife.

The poor little mite had tears streaming down her face. Dominic's heart broke for her. Kelly's young mind had obviously chosen denial as a means to cope with what she knew must have happened to her mother.

"Kelly, *ma chère*, how about we get a special headstone made up for her grave and have a memorial service for her? That way, you can say goodbye to your mum. Would you like to do that?"

With a slight nod, Kelly buried her face into Adele's shoulder. Adele pressed her cheek against her hair and began humming to her a French lullaby her mother used to hum to her as a child. Curious, Dominic had quizzed her about the tune before their wedding.

A hand on his shoulder brought his attention to his younger brother. Conner looked stressed and worn out, not like his usual carefree self at all.

"What's up, Conner?"

"So much. Too much. Want to go for a run?"

"Sounds good. The girls could use some time without us males around, I'm sure."

He glanced over to Adele, who was watching him and nodded that she'd heard. Grabbing his keys out of his pocket, he followed Conner out to the Rav 4, to head deep into the Cradle Mountains where they could run in their snow leopard forms without risk of being seen.

As they drove, he sensed Conner's needed to talk.

"So, what's got you looking so strung out?"

"My mate turned twenty-one while you were gone."

"Ahh, and you're desperate to find her already? Know that feeling."

Dominic shook his head slightly. Trust his little brother to get so worked up about not knowing-

"Oh, I know precisely who she is. She's here in town."

The car swerved slightly as the shock hit Dominic. "Who?"

"Tina Anderson. You probably didn't hear about what happened at the hairdressers the morning of your wedding."

Adele had told him about the young woman in the wheelchair so he cut his brother short, anxious to get to the real issue, "Adele told me what happened."

"Okay. Well, that's Tina, in the chair. But she's basically being held prisoner. I don't know what to do, Dom. We were secretly meeting at night, but Robyn found out and now, all we have is Dream Bonding." Conner let out a long suffering sigh. "In our last dream she tried to kill herself. I got there in time to save her. But what if she does something like that in the real world?"

Dominic's mind whirled. Sympathy for his brother, and for Tina, coursed through him.

"I'm guessing simply taking her is out of the question?"

"The only way to do that would be to break in at night and kidnap her. Knowing what I do about Robyn, she'll come looking with the police and I'll be charged and locked up. Then who will help her? I can't risk it. Especially with her state of mind as it is. She might see it as me kidnapping her and never forgive me. Trust me, Dom, I've thought long and hard about it. Even offered to take her that first night we met up, but she shut me down, saying she didn't know me well enough to run away with me."

"I'm so sorry, bro. I'll have to think about it and you need to tell me everything. I'm sure between all of us we can come up with something."

"I'll fill you in on everything after. I really need to run right now."

"I completely understand. Adele and I got to run in the Tibetan mountains with Choden. It was awesome."

"Wow. That would definitely be an experience of a lifetime."

Conner perked up as Dominic filled him in on some of the lighter moments of their trip. Dominic would do anything to ease his younger brother's pain.

Chapter Five

Tina felt hollow, strangely detached from herself. She was on edge too, unable to concentrate on anything. She checked through the curtain for the hundredth time since she'd arrived with Robyn. Finally, both Barbara and Robyn had clients. Quietly, she wheeled out of the salon's back door. It had been three days since she'd seen Conner, outside of her dreams. Conner had told her they were real, but she wasn't sure it was true. Even if they were real, it would never be enough to only be able to be near him a few hours each night.

Robyn had now restricted her life to the point it felt as though she was suffocating. Her chest ached and she was tired, both in body and mind. So much so, that this morning she could barely muster the energy required to get out of bed. It didn't help that she now had to wait for Robyn to bring in her chair.

Once out on the street, Tina headed to the firehouse hoping to find Conner. Something deep within her was calling out for him, craving his touch, wanting to be near him and needing to obtain that feeling of being protected that she only felt when in his arms. It took fifteen minutes but she made it. *Damn it.* The door was locked.

Frowning, she moved to the larger roller-door of the vehicle bay. Looking though the row of clear plastic panels centered in the red metal, she felt her heart sink. Empty. He must be out on a job.

She simply stared at the red door as her mind crashed, the ache in her chest turned to agony and tears streamed down her face.

She just couldn't go on like this.

In a low pain-filled whisper, she spoke aloud to no one, "A prisoner who is in constant pain. That's my life in a nutshell."

And how sad was that?

Her leg still ached most days, but the real pain was deep inside. She felt so alone. Her mother's rejection was still a fresh wound on her heart. Her father had now abandoned her too—she understood he needed to work, but it didn't change the fact that it left her alone. All her friends in Sydney had quickly forgotten her. She felt totally deserted.

She slowly rolled back toward the salon. Distractedly she watched a bus turn onto the road beside her, heading toward her. Maybe...if she simply checked out of life, she wouldn't be in pain. It would be gone. Robyn wouldn't be able to use her anymore. All her problems would be solved. With a heavy heart she allowed the bus to pass her, a breeze washing over her as it did. Could she do it?

"Dad would miss me, but I'm sure he'd recover."

He'd not been a part of her life for so long he'd quickly adjust to not having her around again. Her damn mother would no doubt be relieved. *Conner*. She sighed as she closed her eyes and pictured him. He was so handsome. He'd been so mad at her in that dream when she'd tried to end it all. But that was just a dream. She couldn't be certain he truly felt for her like that. He'd turned into a damn snow leopard. That couldn't be real.

Conner is a fantasy, one that's not destined to ever be mine.

As the fresh heartache ripped through her, she opened her eyes and focused on a delivery van coming up the road. She gripped her wheels tightly, waiting for the perfect moment. With a couple of hard and fast pushes, she hurtled off the footpath and into the oncoming traffic.

Tires squealed seconds before her chair spun and she was thrown free. Pain radiated through her left side, her shoulder and bicep burned as the asphalt scraped her skin from her body.

"What the fuck? Tina? Tina!"

A panicked female voice she knew from somewhere came closer, continuing to cuss and scream her name. She glanced over to see flame-red hair. Kit, the one who delivered Conner's present.

"I've called the ambulance. I didn't see her till it was too late. What the hell was she thinking?" The man spoke as he ran to her side. Tina assumed he was the driver. Tina closed her eyes against them both, ignoring their conversation. Tears flowed freely. She was such a bloody failure. She couldn't even do this right. Now she was more broken than before, in more pain. She knew for certain Robyn would chain her to the desk now, taking the last shred of freedom from her. She sobbed harder as she realized that all she'd accomplished was to make her life worse.

Conner dropped to his knees as agony ripped through him. He'd been feeling off all morning, but this sudden attack left him breathless. Dominic snatched the hose from his clenched fist and turned the flow off before handing it to Joel who'd also come over to check on him.

"It has to be Tina. She's hurt. Bad."

Dominic frowned down at him for a moment. "I know you want to go to her, but you're in no state to run back into town, and this grass fire isn't big but we can't leave it."

Conner ripped out his phone when it started ringing. "Kit."

"And Adele is calling me, this can't be good."

No, it couldn't be good. Adele was Rosebery's paramedic so her involvement meant an ambulance had been called. He turned from his brother to answer Kit's call.

"What happened, Kit? I can feel her pain."

"I'm sorry, Conner, but it looks like she tried to kill herself."

His heart clenched. "She tried to- is she okay?"

Conner's hands began to tremble as he waited for Kit's response.

"Physically, she'll recover."

"How?" Conner was having trouble breathing. His mate had tried to take her own life, again. Visions of her standing atop the waterfall in their dream flashed through his mind.

"She was watching traffic, she looked dazed. She'd come to the station but left when she saw the vehicle bay was empty. I'd just arrived when I caught sight of her turning away from the door. I went after her to see if she was okay. Before I realized what she was planning on doing, she'd pushed herself onto the road, straight in front of a delivery van. It swerved, but still clipped her chair and she was thrown free. Her left side is all scraped to shit from hitting the road. Adele came and we're on the way to the hospital now. Where are you?"

"We're out at a grass fire, at least twenty minutes away from you. Fuck, Kit. What the hell am I supposed to do?"

"Personally, I vote we go tie up Robyn and beat the shit out of her. Selfish fucking bitch."

Conner couldn't help but grin at Kit's words. He loved Kit like a sister and he fully understood how she felt. He felt the same way. "I wish, but she isn't worth the trouble. Look, we've nearly got this fire out so I'll head in once we're finished. You'll stay with her, right? Don't you dare leave her alone with Robyn."

Conner shuddered at the thought of Tina, injured as she was, being alone with Robyn.

"You don't have to ask, Conner. You know me better than that. No way in hell will that bitch lay a finger on her while I'm there."

"Yeah, I know. Just needed to say it. Okay, I'll be there as soon as I can. Bye, Kit."

"See you then."

Conner hung up and rubbed his chest. His heart ached. But he felt a measure of reassurance now that Kit was with her. Tina would be safe until he could make it to her. Ignoring the fire, he went to the vehicle to grab a bottle of water and sit on the ledge at the back of the truck for a minute. Until he got himself under wraps he was useless to the team. The pain he'd felt rip through his body had now dimmed to almost non-existent. He guessed that meant Tina was now unconscious.

Connor watched Dom jog over to him as guilt swamped him. He should have tried harder to get her free of Robyn. He should have known she'd try something like this after the dream. His eyes stung with unshed tears as Dom reached his side.

"Adele's got her, bro. She's in good hands."

"I know. Kit told me what happened. This is the second time, Dom. I *have* to do something. Maybe I could just take her and run away somewhere. We're both adults, Robyn can't really do anything to stop us."

"That's not a long term solution, and you know it. What about her father? What about us? Your family? Friends? Look, I know Dad's been trying to get in touch with Dale. He hasn't been able to find what company he's now working with. With Tina being in the hospital, he has to be contacted. Clint or Adele will be ringing him. Then he'll know about what's happening, and we can explain what Robyn's been up to. Get Tina out of her care. Hell, if Dale still wants her to have a caretaker, mum will step in."

Conner took a deep breath and finished off his water. That was why Dom was a future alpha; cool and calm under any circumstance, and he made good points.

"Okay, I hadn't thought of any of that. Thanks, Dom. Now, let's get this fire out so I can go see my woman."

With a nod, Dom led him back toward the fire.

It took another half hour to get the fire completely out and mopped up. It had been a small fire, lit on the roadside by some moron flicking a cigarette butt out a window. Thankfully, it had been called in quickly so not much area had burned. Driving back to the station, his muscles grew tense. He honestly didn't know how to quickly get his mate to trust him enough to allow him to take her away from Robyn. He needed her in his arms.

Where she belonged.

Where he could protect her.

The second the truck stopped in the station house, he jumped from the back and headed into the locker room. He showered in record breaking time before he headed out to his Prado.

Ten minutes later Connor rushed through the front doors of the hospital. He'd rung Kit in the car so he knew where to find his mate and headed straight to her room, not stopping for anyone. His steps faltered as he entered her room. Kit and Adele stood beside her bed. Adele was filling out something on a chart. Tina had turned her face away. She looked out the window but her eyes were barely open. Her skin appeared dull, her hair limp. Depression was a ghastly disease, one which had its claws firmly embedded in his precious mate.

"She's been sedated, Conner. We had to calm her down. It was the only way we could get her shoulder back in place. She's a lucky girl to only have a dislocated shoulder from a run-in with a van."

Conner couldn't form words. His chest ached as he took in the bright white bandages covering her left arm. Oblivious to Kit and Adele's presence, he crumpled to his knees beside her, tears burning his eyes as he pressed his face against her right palm, her cold flesh against his hot skin searing him.

"Why baby? Why'd you try to leave me?"

Wiping her sweaty palms on the crisp linen of her pants, Robyn licked her dry lips as she paced her shop. Tina was missing. Had been for at least an hour. Where would she have gone? Her body stilled as the obvious slammed into her. Of course, she'd seek out that boy.

"Barbara, Conner's a firefighter, right?"

"Sure is, you think she went up to see him?"

She snatched up her keys. "I'll soon find out."

Before she got out the back door, her phone rang. Pulling it out, she saw the number was international. Fuck. The one time Dale calls her, Tina's missing.

"Hello, Robyn speaking."

"What the hell is going on, Robyn? I just got an urgent phone call from the hospital about Tina. Her chair was hit by a van—while she was still in it. Am I not paying you enough to keep my daughter safe?"

"Ah, hi Dale. I'm not sure what's going on. I, ah, was about to go look for her. I only just realized she'd snuck out without letting me know where she was going."

"She *snuck* out? She is an adult, Robyn. You are not supposed to be keeping her locked away. No bloody wonder she's suffering depression!"

"Oh, don't be silly, Dale. I would never lock her away." Although the thought was tempting right about now, "I simply meant she went out without letting me know. I was getting worried for her. Did the hospital tell you she's suffering depression?"

"Yeah, they did. Said a witness saw her roll in front of the van on purpose. Why didn't you bother to inform me that she wasn't doing well?"

Robyn was flustered, how could she answer? "I, ah, hadn't noticed any change in her myself. She kept it well hidden, Dale."

"Whatever. I'm doing what I can to cut short my contract so I can come home. I should never have left her. I'll only need you to continue to look after her until I can get back. Hopefully it won't take long."

"Sure, Dale, Tina's a pleasure to care for. Now, I need to run along and get down to the hospital right away to see how she is."

"Okay, keep me informed, Robyn. No excuses. Bye."

With a low growl, she thrust her phone back in her pocket.

"What is it, Robyn?"

"The stupid girl got herself run over by a van. She's at the hospital. They rung Dale claiming she is suffering *depression* of all things. You'll be all right to close the salon tonight? I have to go deal with this mess."

"Sure, let me know how it goes."

Without responding to Barbara, she headed out to her car, rage building with each and every step. How dare she! Now Dale was mad at her when it wasn't her fault. Damn it. She needed Dale to fall in love with her, not be out for her blood.

Within fifteen minutes she was at the hospital. Marching in with shoulders back and head held high, she demanded at the front desk to be taken to Tina. The receptionist told her the room number and how to get there with no offer to show her. How rude. With a huff, she headed in the direction indicated by the stuffy nurse. She easily found Tina's room and went to enter when a tall muscular female stepped into the doorway, blocking her entry.

"Get out of my way."

"I don't think so. There is no way in hell I'm letting you near Tina."

Robyn eyed the woman from her flame-red hair to her bright red boots. Her muscled arms crossed over her chest, her legs shoulder width apart. This woman was a fighter. No way would Robyn be able to physically push past her. She'd have to talk her way into the room.

"I am her caretaker. I have every right to be here. Who are you? What right do *you* have?"

The woman before her growled and bared her teeth, with her slightly slanted eyes she looked every inch a predator, but Robyn refused to be intimidated by her.

"Cat got your tongue? I said, who are you?"

A cold laugh was her response. "This cat will take more than your tongue. I'm no one you want to mess with, bitch. Now, get out of here before I forget where I am."

The hairs on the back of Robyn's neck stood up at the waves of malevolence that radiated from this woman. Robyn looked past her into the room, and her body stiffened. None other than Conner White knelt by Tina's bedside with his head pressed into her hand.

"What is he doing here? He has no right!"

"*He* has every right to be exactly where he is. Last warning. Get of here."

"Or what? What are you going to do? I am her legal guardian, appointed by her father. She will be coming home with me just as soon as she's released."

"Oh honey, I wouldn't tempt me like that. I may just decide to screw the consequences and take you outside for a bit. I guarantee it would be a lesson you'd never forget. And we'll just wait and see who takes Tina home when she's well."

With a loud huff, Robyn turned on her heel and headed away from the room. She needed to find the boss of this place. Surely he'd see reason and remove these two from Tina's room. How convenient it was that the poor girl was mentally unstable with her depression. With Tina being over eighteen and legally an adult, the only way Robyn could use the Medical Power of Attorney was if Tina was either unconscious and in need of medical treatment or if she was of 'unsound mind.'

Conner's tears branded Tina's soul. She'd just wanted a moment's peace. A time when she didn't hurt. Instead, her impulsive decision had caused more pain. She'd never intended to hurt Conner. She honestly hadn't known he truly cared for her. She'd thought he saw her as the poor cripple who needed his compassion. But this reaction spoke of deeper emotion. Here was a tough six foot two man crying over her. His hot tears filled her palm. She couldn't deny his feelings must be deep and true.

She'd turned away from the door toward the window when they'd settled her into this bed. The morphine had kicked in fully now, making her body heavy and unresponsive. She wanted to see Conner, wanted to turn her face toward him. She focused her energy and moved her head smoothly over so she could see his glossy black hair against the white sheet and her pale arm.

"I'm sorry." Her speech was slurred and whisper quiet but he'd heard. His head popped up from the bed, and his watery red eyes held her gaze.

"Why, baby?" His voice cracked with pain,

splintering her heart.

"I hurt. All the time. Just want…some peace."

Tears slid down her face. The emotion in his gaze reflected her own, making it too much for her to contain. He rose up from where he'd been kneeling by her side. Callused thumbs tenderly wiped the moisture away before he cupped her face. He took her mouth in a kiss so fiercely possessive it left his imprint on her soul.

"I'll fix this. I'll find a way to get you away from Robyn. Even if we have to leave-"

Footsteps outside her room stopped Conner from finishing. Tina glanced at the door to see who was entering. A doctor strode in, his short brown hair messy as if he'd been running his hands through it. He had kind hazel eyes and a gentle smile. Her lips twitched, trying to return his smile. Conner greeted the doctor with an ease that had to mean they'd known each other for some time.

"Hi Doc."

"Hi Conner, Tina, it's good to see you awake." He came closer to the bed to shake Conner's hand, before he sighed and crossed his arms. "We've got problems. Adele's told me about the situation. We've reported the incident as an accident, not the suicide attempt it really was. This keeps the police out of it. Do not make me regret covering for you, understand?"

Tina gave a slight nod as Conner agreed with the doctor, assuring him he'd keep a very close eye on her from now on. A warmth spread through her at his words, a warmth that soon dissipated at the doctor's next words.

"Robyn is causing a stink, as I'm sure you're both aware she would. She claims to have a Medical Power of Attorney for you, Tina. I refused to do anything until she produces it, but once she does, my hands are tied. I spoke to your father earlier this morning and he's currently doing everything he can to get back to you, but it's not going to be anytime soon. He has to get out of his contract, then arrange transport off the rig." He paused to rub the bridge of his nose. "Kit verbally abused and threatened Robyn with physical violence. I understand her reasoning, but Kit can't pull that crap—especially on hospital grounds. Conner, will you talk to her?"

"Sure, Clint. Not sure it will do any good. Kit's protective of us all. You know her well enough to know she wouldn't ever start something here in the hospital unless she absolutely had to."

"Yeah, I know. But Robyn could report her to the police and get her charged. I'd hate to see Kit earn a record over this. Now, from what Adele has told me, Tina hasn't been getting the rehab required for her leg to recuperate. Is that right?"

"She won't help. Refuses." Tina's voice was still slurred, but both men seemed to be able to understand her broken speech.

"Okay. I'll have the hospital physio come in to assess you. She'll show you and Conner what you need to do. Now, even though we didn't report the suicide attempt, you have been diagnosed with depression. Unfortunately it means Robyn can activate the Medical Power of

Attorney, if she does in fact have one. She's claiming the depression is affecting your ability to make sound decisions, Tina. I'll do my best to keep you here till your dad gets back, but I can't guarantee it, especially if Robyn finds that document. I'll be sending our psychiatrist in to talk to you too. She'll need to assess what we can do to help you. She may also be able to help us get around that damn Power of Attorney."

A knock on the doorframe drew all their attention.

"Ahh, Nina, perfect timing. Conner, Tina, this is Nina, our physio. I'll leave you three to get started. Either of you need anything, just get the nurses to buzz me, okay?"

"Shall do, Clint. And thanks for all your help. Appreciate it."

"No trouble, Conner. Let's hope we can get things sorted in time."

With that, Clint left the room. Tina's mind clouded a little. All these people who barely knew her were willing to do so much to help her. Before she could become too overwhelmed, Nina caught her attention.

"Okay guys, so as the good doctor said, I'm Nina and I'm here to help you get back on your feet. I've tracked down your medical records and know what was suggested. It all sounds good to me, so I'll spend some time going through it all and make sure you both know how to do each exercise properly. Sound good?"

Tears welled in Tina's eyes. It sounded better than good. Conner gripped her hand in his before he responded.

"That would be great."

Tina's mind whirled with everything that was suddenly happening. For over an hour Nina explained and demonstrated exercises. Some she could do on her own, but some she'd need assistance with. Conner was enthusiastic, wanting to help her however he could. Watching him listening intently, before laying his hands on her leg to aid her, made her smile. Her muscles were beginning to ache from all the movement but her heart felt lighter. She struggled to keep the wince of pain from her face as Conner arranged her leg flat on the mattress.

"I think we'll call it a day. I'll get the nurse to give you another shot of morphine to help with the pain. If you need me to go through anything again, get the nurses to buzz me for you. I'll be back to check in on you in a few days, in any case."

Nina left and moments later a nurse came in and administered the shot. Then she was alone with Conner. He pulled a chair over to her bed and sat there stroking her face and hair. The drug began to make her mind feel fuzzy, sleepy. But before she passed out, she had to know. "Why? Why are you here?"

"Because I love you, Tina, my precious mate."

The words were a low whisper. She wasn't sure if they'd been real or in her head as she slipped into her pain free, drug hazy sleep.

Chapter Six

Conner paced up and down the hospital corridor in an attempt to vent some of his nervous energy. Dominic had taken him off the roster so he could spend as much time with Tina as possible. The last three days had been pretty good, all things considered. He'd spent all his time at the hospital. That small fold-out couch was uncomfortable as all get out, but the discomfort was worth being able to spend every moment with his mate.

"Mr White?"

Conner spun on his heel and strode to where the psychiatrist stood several steps away from Tina's door. She'd been in with Tina for a bloody long time, long enough that he'd had time to race home for a shower and change of clothes.

"Since when have I been *Mr White*, Jennifer? First names are fine."

"Fair enough. Well, Tina has given me permission to discuss her case with you. There are a number of things that concern me." Conner bet there were more than a couple. Dr Jennifer Reid was also a snow leopard shifter, except she was like his dad—one of the rare shifters with enhanced abilities. His dad was strongly empathic. He would often be sick when he was around people emitting intense emotions. Jennifer could read emotion and intentions. While she couldn't actually read thoughts, she came damn close.

"Things that we need to discuss in private." She raised her hand to stop him interrupting her. "I know you don't want her left alone. I've got Adele coming to sit with her."

"Okay, but I'm not leaving her until Adele gets here. I won't leave her alone, not when we don't know where Robyn is."

"I fully understand your concerns, Conner. Here she comes now."

With a quick nod and smile, Adele slipped into Tina's room.

"Hi Tina, how about I help you have a shower?" Adele's voice floated out of the room as Jennifer led him down the hall toward her office.

Once they'd both settled into seats, Jennifer didn't waste any time.

"Tina is your mate, correct?"

"Yeah, she is."

"You need to get her away from Robyn. The sooner, the better. Tina will never recover, physically or mentally, while under her care. I have no idea what her father was thinking putting his daughter in her care in the first place. Robyn is a hairdresser. She has no experience or training to be a caretaker for anyone, let alone a fragile young woman grappling with a life altering injury. I can only guess it was a hasty decision made out of desperation.”

“I know how destructive Robyn is to Tina, but I can’t even see Tina when she’s in Robyn’s care. The only contact I’ve had before her hospitalization was through Dream Bonding. I’m getting so strung out, Jennifer. I need to have her safe and in my arms.”

“So marry her. If you get married, Robyn has no say. As her husband, her care is in your hands. It stinks she doesn’t have more control of her own life at the moment. She is legally an adult. But if Robyn has a Medical Power of Attorney, she can make decisions in regard to Tina’s health. Normally, there are clauses which dictate that only if Tina is either unconscious or mentally unsound, Robyn gains control. With Tina’s depression, it leaves the door wide open for Robyn to take advantage.”

“What about her dad? Can he revoke the power of attorney? Surely, his rights as her parent supersede Robyn’s?”

“I’m not familiar with the inner workings of the legal system, but Dale isn’t here, so it’s a moot point. My advice is for you to propose to her. Looking at the reports of her condition, both physical and mental, from admission to now—just three days later—she’s improved a great deal. She feels the connection with you and is blossoming under your love and care. But we can’t keep her cooped up in here. A major part of her depression is because she feels trapped, like she’s being held prisoner. That’s not going to improve while she’s stuck in a hospital bed."

Conner knew Jennifer was speaking the truth. He just wasn't ready to lose what they'd built these last days. But her idea of proposing had merit. Hopefully Tina knew him well enough now to say yes.

"I'm not sure she'll say yes if I propose. She's only known me for a few weeks."

"Well, I suggest you spend the next couple of days wisely. I can't see Tina staying past the weekend. You'll have until then. Otherwise, sadly, Tina will be going back to live with Robyn."

Conner said his goodbyes and wandered back down to Tina's room, his heart heavy. How could he convince her in just a few days to marry him? And as her fiancé, could he stop Robyn from taking her? He stood in the doorway and watched his mate. Adele had produced some nail polish from somewhere and was painting Tina's toenails. The soft pink color suited her dainty feet. He looked up to her face to see her watching him with a smile. He moved to her side as he forced down his worries.

"Hey there, baby doll." He leaned in for a kiss before pulling back. "You ladies having a mini spa day or something?"

"Something like that," Adele winked at Tina. "However, I better be getting back to work. I'll see you later, Tina. You too, Conner."

Conner settled into the chair by Tina's side as Adele left them alone, closing the door behind her. Unable to not touch his mate, he stroked her face. He barely held back his purr as she nuzzled into his palm. He wasn't certain she'd believed him about the shifter thing in their dream , and he didn't want to freak her out.

"Your hair's damp. Did you go home?"

"Yeah, did a quick run home to shower and change while you were with Dr Reid. Also picked up something for you."

Reaching into his pocket, he pulled free the necklace he'd previously given her.

"Like I told you, I found it outside your window. I've had the chain fixed. Mum suggested making it longer. Now you can hide it under your shirt so Robyn won't see it."

"Oh, thank you, Conner. I've missed wearing it."

She reached forward and fingered the heart before Conner leaned over and clasped it around her neck.

"The only time you've mentioned the broken chain was in my dream."

She whispered the words as a frown came down over her face.

"You didn't believe me when I told you I was really there, did you?"

"It was a dream, Conner. My fantasy come to life. I *wanted* you to be real. How can I believe it when my imagination could easily have come up with it? And walking in another's dreams, is...insane. It can't be real."

"Tina, it's all real. I am real. My love for you is very real. The dreams we share are called Dream Bonding. Only possible between a shifter and his destined mate."

Conner watched as Tina's face showed her every emotion as she tried to come to grips with everything.

"Shifter. You- you expect me to believe that you turn into a big cat? Whenever you feel like it?"

He smiled as she cocked her brow at him.

"Sure do. Would you like a demonstration?"

"You're serious aren't you?"

"One hundred percent."

Conner could see the war going on behind Tina's emerald gaze. He stripped his shirt over his head and purred at her gasp. Unbuttoning his pants, he watched her eyes widen.

"What are you doing?"

"I'll shred my clothes if I shift in them. I need to strip first."

"But, in the dream, you had clothes after you shifted."

"Yeah, that was a trick in the dream. Real world doesn't work that way, unfortunately."

He continued to strip, thoroughly enjoying the blush that spread over her cheeks and down her neck as he revealed all of himself to his mate. With a sly grin, he called to his leopard, feeling the energy envelop him. Then he was gazing up at his rather shocked looking mate from his leopard's eyes. He padded slowly toward her, purring loudly. She pushed herself up in the bed, shying away from him. He lowered his head and whined. He didn't want her scared. He lowered himself down next to her bed and laid his head between his paws. He looked up at her, begging with his gaze that she accept him.

As the snow leopard lay still on the floor near her, Tina slowly relaxed from where she'd pushed up against the top of the bed. Conner was really a snow leopard. She rubbed her eyes, blinking to clear her vision.

He was still a cat, so she hadn't been hallucinating.

Very slowly, Tina slid from the bed, the cold of the floor seeping into the soles of her feet, letting her know this wasn't another dream. She gripped the mattress tightly but couldn't prevent her legs giving out under her. As she crumpled, heading for a hard landing on the floor, the animal moved forward. She curled her hands through the thick fur on his neck as he pressed his large head against her tummy and lowered her gently to the floor with a small growl. It wasn't loud enough to scare her, but the message he wasn't impressed at her hurting herself was clear.

She'd wondered if he'd know her in this form, obviously he did. Just like in her dream, he'd saved her from harm. She arranged herself on the floor before reaching a hand out toward him. He tilted his massive head to press the top of it into her touch. *So soft*. Her breath hitched as she threaded her fingers deep into his thick coat. Purring, he nuzzled his face into her lap.

"You're real. You're really a snow leopard. And a man. How is this possible? I don't understand."

The huge animal stood, and after delivering a playful lick to her cheek stepped away from her before the ball of blue light engulfed him once more, and Conner the man reappeared. She didn't move as he pulled his pants back on and slowly prowled toward her. He scooped her easily from the floor and sat on the bed with her on his lap. He stroked her hair behind her ears and kissed the edge of her mouth.

"There is a legend that explains our creation. Would it help you understand to hear it?"

She stroked her fingertips down Conner's smooth cheek. He'd obviously shaved when he'd gone home earlier. "I imagine it would help. Could you please tell me?"

"Okay, here goes. This is going to test my memory. Back in 1759 an old Tibetan monk and his young student realized the snow leopards were rapidly being hunted to extinction. They both spent a lot of time researching ways to save the animals. You see, the monks and snow leopards had lived in harmony for a long time. Many of the monks had a close bond with an individual snow leopard. So when they found a solution, a way to combine a man with a beast, the young monk and his animal volunteered. Under the light of a new moon, the elder monk cast the spell. The magic worked, fusing together the two to form the first shifter. That wasn't the end of it, though. The magic was stronger than they had anticipated. Also, unbeknown to them, Halley's Comet was passing overhead at the time. The spell was strengthened by the comet, and also formed a bond with it. Along with Choden, the first shifter, a pair of mated shifters were conceived that night on each continent. Now, every time Halley's Comet passes Earth, another mated pair is conceived on each continent."

"Mated pair? I'm fairly certain my birth doesn't line up with Halley's Comet, Conner."

"No, baby doll. You're all human, don't worry. Each of those pairs went on to have families. I'm part of one of those families. Often, male shifters are aligned with a human mate. For some unknown reason, there are more male shifters born than females."

"So, I'm your *mate*? How do you know for certain?"

He nuzzled his face into her neck, inhaling against her skin. Goose bumps rose all over her body in response.

"The night before your twenty-first birthday we shared a dream, do you remember?"

"Of course I do. You saved me. You stopped my nightmares. I haven't had one since."

"Hmm, good to hear. Well, just before that one, I had a different dream. You see, a male shifter will see visions of his mate in his sleep, starting on her twenty-first birthday. I saw your white-blond hair, then a flash of your stunning emerald eyes, followed by the spokes of your wheelchair. Most shifters can't tell from their first dream who their mate is. It can take decades for a male to find his mate from the hints he gets while he's sleeping. But I knew. Instantly, I knew it was you."

He pulled away from her neck and cradled her head in his palms.

"You are my mate, Tina. I love you and I will protect

you forever. Please say yes." He finished off with a whisper and she frowned at his words. He hadn't asked any questions, what did he want her to say yes to?

"Tina, baby doll, would you marry me? Will you let me keep you safe and protected for the rest of our lives?"

Marriage! Tina felt her eyes widen in shock, every drop of moisture in her mouth evaporate. She examined Conner's face intently. She detected no lies, no hidden agenda. His blue-gray gaze looked full of adoration with a touch of concern. He said he loved her, but did she love him? Could she marry when she wasn't sure? Look what happened to her parents. No. She was not her mother. She would never treat Conner in such a way. Surely love would grow? And it did mean an escape from Robyn...

"Breathe, baby. Deep breaths."

Stars played at the edge of her vision as she sucked in air. She hadn't been aware she was holding her breath.

"Sorry, I was so caught up in my mind I forgot to breathe for a moment."

Taking another deep breath and wetting her dry lips, she ran her fingertip down his nose and across his mouth. Leaning in, she kissed Conner softly before pulling away just a fraction.

"I'm not certain I love you, Conner. I care for you. A lot. I can't deny the connection we have. I love the way you make me feel, the way you care for me."

"That bitch has made you doubt your worth. Look in your heart, Tina. Deep in your heart and soul, you know what I say is the truth. I. Love. You. And you are worthy of my love. I know you love me too. You just need some time to realize it yourself. I'll give you all the time you need, and I wish I didn't have to force this decision on you so early in our relationship, but I can't let Robyn continue to destroy you. You've tried twice now to end it all. I can't live in a world where you don't. Please, baby doll, allow me to protect and care for you. Say yes."

Closing her eyes against the tears that were flowing freely over her cheeks, she pressed her lips to his again, more of an intimate touch rather than a kiss.

"Yes, Conner. To all of it. Yes."

With a groan, Conner took over the kiss, hot, needy and passionate. He ate her alive. Her body burned for him. His hard erection rubbed over her hip as she continued to sit on his lap. As she felt heat bloom between her thighs, he pulled back with a sharp inhale.

"Someone's coming."

Leaving her on the bed, he raced over to his clothes and quickly finished redressing. Tina was in awe, his supernatural speed amazing to watch. He could have left his shirt off though. His chest was a work of art.

She heard footsteps outside the door as Conner came back to her, scooping her up in his arms. There was a sharp knock on the door moments before Dr Maynard came into the room.

"Ah, so you're up and looking much healthier, Tina. Do you mind if you hop back into bed so I can check your vitals?"

Tina grinned as Conner settled her on the bed with a

tender kiss to her cheek. He really was too good to be true. Her very own knight in shining armor had ridden in to save her. Or rather, prowled in as a cat and saved her.

"Hey kiddo, how would you like to come shopping with me again?"

He grinned as Kelly sat up straighter.

"What are we buying this time?"

"I need a very special something this time. Can you keep a secret, Kelly?"

"I'm thirteen years old, Uncle Conner. Of course I can keep a secret."

He chuckled at her as he leaned in to whisper in her ear, "I asked Tina to marry me and she said yes."

Kelly squealed and wrapped her arms around Conner's neck to hug him. His ears rung from her pitch but he didn't mind. After the years of abuse she'd lived through, watching her be so happy was worth it.

"Awesome! I get to be a bridesmaid again."

He pulled back and tapped her nose. "Trust you to think of that. Cheeky girl."

"So you want to go back to the jewelry shop? For a ring?"

"Precisely. Think you can help me find one that's perfect? You know she loves the pendant you helped me pick out."

Before Conner could get the keys out of his pocket, Kelly had raced toward his green Prado. With a shake of his head, he followed her.

Ten minutes later they pulled up outside Rosebery Jewels. With Kelly all but vibrating with excitement, they headed into the store. Conner was pretty sure he would have been able to select the perfect ring for Tina on his own, but Kelly had enjoyed their last trip here so much he wanted her to share the experience. That, and being able to give the kid good memories to replace all those shitty ones, was a good feeling.

"I think it needs a green stone. To match her eyes."

Kelly's memory astounded him. "You really do remember her from that one time you've seen her, don't you?"

"Of course I do. I told you before, the sadness I saw in her eyes was what used to be in mine. Not something I forget when I see it. That, and they were such a pretty green."

"Well, I agree. Her eyes are a stunning emerald green."

"But you still have to have diamonds on it, Uncle Conner. A girl has to have diamonds."

He chuckled, even though he fully agreed Tina's ring needed diamonds. "You've been watching too much TV, young lady."

He regretted his words the moment they left his mouth as he watched her face drop.

"TV was all I had."

Shit. Now I've really put my foot in it.

"I know, Kelly. I didn't really mean it, I was just mucking around. I'm sorry."

He pulled her into his chest and gave her a tight hug before releasing her. The action still felt awkward, he'd never done emotion well. Except with Tina. With her, it was as natural as breathing. A tug on his hand pulled him from his thoughts.

"Oh! It's perfect, come see, Uncle Conner."

He followed where Kelly's finger pointed with his gaze and sucked in his breath. It was perfect. A white gold setting with a large oval emerald in the center, flanked by two brilliant cut diamonds with a couple of diamond chips inlaid around them. The thing that really set the ring off was the thin white gold band that curled over above the emerald. The ring looked modern, yet elegant. Tina would love it, he was certain.

"You nailed it again, Kelly. That is the perfect choice for Tina."

He caught the attention of a sales assistant and made quick work of the purchase.

He couldn't wipe the grin from his face. He had a fiancé. His mate was soon going to be his. He glanced at Kelly who sat in the passenger seat. She was holding the ring box open and turning it so the sun would glint off the gems in different ways.

"What are you doing there?"

"Just seeing all the different angles and lines. The ring looks fabulous, but when you just look at a small part, like this little bit here"—she pointed to the intricate setting that held the diamonds in place—"it's still brilliant. Every little bit of it."

His brain ran a mile a minute. Kelly liked art? He knew Adele had been searching for hobbies for her to get involved with. Art was an easy one to accommodate. He'd been a fairly decent artist in his teen years. He turned the car down a side street to head toward an art supply shop he'd not been in since he left school.

As he pulled up, Kelly put away the ring and looked around. "Where are we? What else do you need to get?"

"This stop isn't for me. It's for you."

"But I don't need anything."

The little frown on her face was cute, but he didn't like her worried.

"The way you described Tina's ring a moment ago, it gave me an idea. I think you might enjoy getting into art. So, I thought a good first step would be some sketching stuff. I used to draw a lot. I can help you get started if you like. I know you'll get the hang of it in no time."

"You think I'd be good at it?"

"With practice, I'm sure you'll be amazing at it."

"You don't have to buy me things."

"No, I don't. But I want to. I want to see you smile every day because you're enjoying your life. And, you've helped me impress my girl twice now. Got to say thank you properly. Now, come on. Let's see if we can't set you up with the basics."

Finally! Jake sighed in relief as his email flashed up with a mobile phone number for Dale Anderson. With a quick prayer of thanks he picked up his phone and dialed the number.

"Dale Anderson."

With a rush of relief, Jake sat down at his desk.

"Hey Dale, my name's Jake White. Not sure if you remember me, but we went to school together, back in the day."

"Yeah, sure I remember you. How you doing these days?"

"I'm all good. Listen, I'm not going to beat around the bush with this. I'm ringing about your daughter, Tina."

A long sigh came over the line. "What's happened now?"

"Well, that depends on what you know."

"Not a hell of a lot. I know her wheelchair got hit by a van—with her in it. Other than that, I've just been trying to get back to her. I canned my contract on the rig and am trying to arrange transport to get home. I'm stuck in Sydney airport at the moment. Massive storm has just rolled in so I don't think I'll be there until at least late tonight."

Relief spread through Jake. Dale was nearly here. Jake had feared he was still stuck out on a rig in the middle of the ocean somewhere.

"Okay, well, you let me know what time you're landing and I'll pick you up. Because your daughter needs you, like, yesterday. Not sure if you know, but my youngest son, Conner, has fallen head over heels for young Tina. He hasn't left her side since she was hospitalized."

"Any boy of yours is going to be good for her. Do you know how Tina feels about him?"

Jake let out a deep breath, thankful that Dale was so accepting of Conner. It could be a real mess if Dale was against their relationship. He could have potentially sided with Robyn.

"Not real sure. Robyn has been keeping Tina on lockdown. Barely lets the poor girl out of her sight. Conner's been pressed to just see her. He got a friend, Kit, to sneak a present to her on her birthday. Kit also gave Tina his phone number. They started seeing each other late at night. After Robyn would retire for the evening, Tina would go out the back and chat with him a while before heading back in. But Robyn found out, took Tina's phone and Conner tells me she now takes her chair at night. So she can't leave the house."

"She did what? Bloody hell, as much as I don't like the idea of my baby girl being all grown up, she is. She should be allowed the freedom to date! To leave the house. No wonder she's depressed and the doc's worried about her."

He hated having to be the bearer of bad news but there were things Dale had to know. Rubbing the bridge of his nose, he continued. "Sadly, I believe things are about to get worse."

"How could it?"

"Kit was the first to the scene when the accident happened. Kit's a good woman. Tough as nails but loyal and has the biggest heart. She went to the hospital with

Tina in the ambulance. The medic that attended is my daughter-in-law, so Tina was in good hands. Knowing what they did about how Robyn has been treating your daughter, they asked the doc to ring you, not Robyn. I'm guessing you then rang Robyn?"

"Yeah, rang her to ask her what the hell was going on. Not that it did me any good."

Jake had feared that's what had happened. Not that he could blame Dale. If he were in Dale's place, he was certain he would have done something similar.

"Well, Robyn came storming into the hospital. Kit refused to allow her access to Tina. Then Robyn saw that Conner was by her beside. She went nuts. Tried to get the hospital to remove Conner from her room. Kit got verbal with her and she stormed off, claiming she had a legal document proving her authority as Tina's guardian and that she'd return with it. She hasn't shown up with anything yet, but it's only a matter of time. Do you know what document she's talking about?"

A heavy sigh came over the line. "I thought it was the right thing to do. She is Tina's caretaker, if something happened and urgent decisions needed to be made. Out on the rig, communication is so limited. I needed someone there with her who could make the decisions. I made sure there were clauses in the power of attorney, ones that only allowed Robyn to make decisions if Tina was unable to, what was the wording? Something about being unconscious or of unsound mind. But never did I think it would be used like this! Bloody hell, what have I done to my daughter?"

Suddenly, Jake was very grateful this conversation was happening over the phone. With the level of emotion pouring off Dale, Jake would be struggling not to be sick if they were face to face. As it was, his stomach was churning from the small amount he was transmitting through his voice over the phone line.

"Don't be too hard on yourself, Dale. All any of us can do is our best. You did yours. Still are. You got word Tina's in trouble, and you immediately hightailed it straight home to be with her. You're a good father."

"Not feeling it just at the moment, mate. Why would Robyn do this? I mean, I know she had a crush on me back in school, that's why I figured she offered. I knew she wasn't trained but I thought it wasn't that big of a job. I mean, Tina's an adult. She just needed a little help with mobility and someone to go through her rehab exercises with her."

"Yeah, from what Conner has said, Robyn has *never* done any rehab with Tina."

"Never? Tina's depression is making more sense. Do you know- did she really roll in front of the van on purpose?"

He took a deep breath before continuing. This was going to hurt Dale. No matter how much Dale needed to know, Jake wished he could spare him from it.

"Kit wasn't just the first on scene. She was running to grab her when it happened. Sorry, Dale. It was definitely on purpose. It hasn't been reported, so the police aren't poking around. Conner told me this morning she's looking a lot better. He's spent every minute he can with her, and he's been working with her on her exercises."

Jake felt for the man on the other end of the phone. Poor bugger, talk about drama. A muffled loud voice came over the phone, Jake couldn't make out words but the cussing coming from Dale made it clear it wasn't good.

"The storm isn't passing any time soon. They've just canceled all domestic flights until the morning. I guess I could hire a car and drive down to Melbourne and catch the ferry across to Tasmania."

"Don't think that'll help. It's a bloody long drive then you'll be stuck waiting for the ferry. It still only runs twice a day. Stay there. Get a good night's sleep and get down here first thing. We'll do whatever we can until you get here."

"Thanks, Jake. I'd better get to a hotel. Guess I'll see you in the morning. I'll text the flight info to you as soon as I have it."

"Sounds like a plan. See you then."

Jake hung up the phone and pressed his fingers into his eyes. He had a really bad feeling about how all this was going to play out. And he hoped like hell that Conner and Tina would both make it out in one piece.

Chapter Seven

A tingle up Tina's spine had her turning to look at the doorway of her hospital room. She'd had a great morning with Kit. They'd played Scrabble and discussed everything from men to music. Then, before Kit left, she insisted Tina learn some self-defense moves. Knowing she was restricted to the chair, Kit spent time showing her pressure points in the arm and leg. Tina was shocked at the drastic effect pressing the right spot on someone could have. She seriously hoped she'd never need to use the knowledge, but it was really sweet of Kit to teach it all to her. But now Kit had gone and she sat bored and alone. Tina hated hospitals. Too much time to sit and think. She'd spent every second since Kit left thinking about Conner. His cheeky smile, muscular physique, and the way he cared for her every need. Conner had spent so much time with her. She knew she was already falling in love with him. But she wasn't ready to admit it to anyone but herself.

"Can't believe I'm doing this for you, bro. You seriously owe me, you know that?"

"I know, Dom. But you of all people understand why I need to do this."

Frowning, she cocked her head to the side, what on earth was Conner up to?

With a raised eyebrow, she watched as Conner slipped into the room and firmly closed the door. With a cheeky sly smile, he prowled over to her—purring the whole way. Her heart rate sped up and tingles ran through her body at the sight he made.

"I bought you something."

"You've already done so much for me, Conner. You didn't need to buy me anything else."

"You said yes."

Her eyes opened wide. He'd bought her a ring? For some reason, she hadn't even thought of it before now. Conner dropped to one knee by her bed and opened his hand to reveal the most stunning emerald ring she'd ever seen.

"Oh, wow. It's beautiful!"

Taking her hand, he slid it on her shaking finger before rising over her and devouring her mouth. Tina wound her hands in his hair—thankful the sling on her arm was now gone. Conner's hands began to roam over her. They glided down her rib cage to the swell of her hips. He bunched up her nightie—the one he'd bought for her—in his fists and moved it up her body. She shuddered as Conner revealed her naked skin to his view, one slow inch at a time. When he reached the lower edge of her breasts, he paused a moment and left her mouth.

"No bra again, baby?"

She nodded, breathless. He lowered his gaze to his

fingers, moments before they kept moving up.

"Arch for me, baby doll."

Without thought, she arched her back and she felt the thin cotton material slip over her nipples, causing them to harden further. Her lids fluttered closed as the garment passed over her head, leaving her naked, aside from her thin cotton knickers. When his touch didn't return immediately to her, she opened her eyes. Her breath froze in her lungs. He was perfection and she would never tire of staring at him. Taut sexy muscles rippled beneath tanned skin as he peeled his shirt over his head. Feeling his gaze on her, she looked up into his sparkling eyes. Her hand came up to touch him on its own accord. He climbed on to the bed and with a knee on either side of her hips he leaned forward, giving her full access to his broad chest.

Her hands played over his flesh. Feeling him tremble beneath her caress sent a zing straight through her. She continued her exploration, her gaze following each stroke her fingers made.

"You are amazing, baby. I've never felt anything as good as your skin against mine. Your touch is driving me insane."

Before Tina could suck in another breath he lowered his body and took a nipple in his mouth. He suckled her gently, slowly building a fire within her. Moving to her other breast, he began laving that one and her body arched under the onslaught. She'd never felt like this—and he'd barely touched her. Her one past lover hadn't been able to stimulate her to climax. Mind you, both times they'd had sex had been while at training camp and they'd snuck off to hide and have some fun.

He groaned as he withdrew his mouth from her skin. She whimpered at the loss of his wet warmth on her flesh. Leaning on his elbows he cradled her face and kissed the life out of her. As he devoured her mouth, his hips began moving. His hard erection encased by the thick material of his pants rubbed against her thin panties in a very delicious way.

Turning her face slightly to break the kiss, she breathed out the words. "Conner, you have to take off your jeans. I need you."

Conner's cheeks were flushed with his arousal as he climbed off the bed, the creaking of the metal reminded her where they were. Snatching the sheet to her, she sat up.

"We can't here! Oh damn. What if someone comes in?"

"Relax, Tina. I have my brother, Dominic, guarding the door for us. Trust me, he won't let anyone in, nor will he take a peek. He's happily married to his mate, Adele."

The tension eased from her muscles, they were safe to enjoy their moment of passion. She dropped the sheet when Conner lowered his jeans, taking his briefs with them. He revealed his body in all its aroused glory to her.

"You're so perfect. Every inch of you." She slid from the bed, leaning against it and Conner moved to stand before her. "Your face is beyond handsome. Your shoulders are strong, wide. And look at your arms. They're so muscular." A shudder ran through her as her hands followed her words. She ran them over his hard abs, enjoying how they rippled beneath her caress. She gripped his hips and lowered herself to her knees. Keeping her pelvis and back straight—she knew Conner wouldn't let her fall. As she took the hard length of him into her mouth, his hands came down to grip her shoulders. She looked up from beneath her lashes and caught his gaze. She ran her tongue over the head, the small taste she licked from him exploding across her senses. He was delicious, his natural scent amplified. Wrapping her grip around his base, she took more of him into her mouth. Loving how he moaned and purred for her as he rocked into her ever so slightly. Releasing him, she took one long lick up the underside of his erection, paying extra attention to the sensitive skin below the head.

An ache settled deep in her womb as his taste filled her and his sounds of arousal surrounded her. He pulled from her mouth and scooped her up from the floor.

"I can smell your need for me, Tina. I will not come for the first time in your mouth. I want to be inside your body."

He laid her gently on the bed and after a quick kiss he set about peeling her panties from her body.

"Your scent is intoxicating." He closed his eyes and took a couple of deep breaths, his body shuddering as he inhaled. Tina began to squirm on the bed. She was beyond turned on and couldn't wait for him to fill her.

Conner had one knee on the bed before he shook his head and with a short growl made his way back to where he'd discarded his pants earlier. He pulled a condom free of the pocket and sheathed himself before returning to her. He prowled up the bed over her, looking decidedly feline.

"I promise I'll be gentle, but you tell me if anything hurts. I don't want to cause any more injury to your hip or leg."

"You won't, Conner. It's so much better with all the rehab you've been helping me with, even though it's only been a few days."

With an expression filled with pride, he ran his hand up the inside of her right thigh and pushed it wide, leaving her injured leg to remain where it was. She moved it as far out as she could comfortably, and he settled into the cradle of her body. Sparks ran through her body as his hot skin came into contact with hers. He lowered his head and caught her mouth in a passionate kiss.

She felt the heat of him moments before his latex covered erection pressed against her. She was so wet and ready for him. Her eyes slid shut as he easily glided into her body. She felt complete with him inside of her, like a puzzle that had found its final piece. Once fully seated, he shuddered above her and buried his face into her neck.

Conner held himself very still. He was buried deep in

his mate's core for the first time. Her tight muscles rippled around him and she tried to move her hips, but he couldn't let her yet. He was too close to the edge. He nipped her neck gently before raising up to speak in her ear.

"Don't move, baby. I need a moment. You feel so good, even in my wildest dreams I couldn't have imagined how good this feels."

She stiffened beneath him slightly and he peppered her face and neck with little kisses.

"You say that like you've never done this before."

"I haven't. I haven't wanted to before you, and I knew you were out there."

"You were waiting for me?"

"Something like that."

Not wanting to lose the moment with talk of virginity, Conner didn't give Tina time to respond. He took her mouth in a passionate kiss at the same time his hips began moving. His first strokes were slow and easy. She felt so good. Her tightness pulled at him as he entered and retreated. She whimpered into his mouth as her grip tightened on his shoulders. Her nails bit into his skin. Not hard enough to break through, but hard enough to let him know exactly how much she was enjoying what they were doing together.

It didn't take long until he couldn't stand the slow pace. Gripping her hips, he thrust harder, faster. Tingling sparks flew throughout his body, racing down his spine. Her muscles were rippling, tightening around him. Heat tore through him as he came inside his mate for the first time with a groan. He did his best to tamp down the noise; the entire hospital didn't need to know what they were doing. The release was so intense, it felt like he was entering paradise and coming home rolled into one.

Tina's fingers threaded into his hair, tilting his head from where it lay on her shoulder. She gently kissed him, feather light caresses that traced his cheekbone down to his mouth. He allowed Tina to control the kiss. She opened up to him so sweetly. He slipped free from her body as he pulled back from her lips. Raising his hand, he ran his fingertips down her face. Part of him still couldn't quite believe she was real and beneath him.

"That was incredible. *You* are incredible."

Her breathy words brought a grin to his face but it soon dropped and his chest tightened as her eyes shone with tears, "I didn't hurt you did I? Was I too rough? Oh damn, your shoulder. I should have been more gentle. I'm sorry, baby doll."

Tina cut him off with a kiss, and unlike her previous gentle one, this was deep and passionate.

"You didn't hurt me, I'm just overwhelmed. What we just did was amazing and the fact you waited for me… What if we didn't meet for another ten years?"

"I would have found you before then. I would have come searching for you. I wouldn't have stopped until I'd found you and I wouldn't have ever strayed with another woman. You have, and always will be, the only one for me."

Conner moved off the bed and scooped Tina up in his arms. He headed toward the bathroom with her securely in his embrace—right where she belonged.

"What are you doing?"

"I'm taking care of my mate, I'm going to wash you clean, then tuck you in. Then I have to go. I've had a lot of time off from the station. Tonight there isn't anyone to cover for me. A lot of the guys headed up to the International Bethotte Rally to help with traffic control and other stuff. Normally, it isn't a problem but you get a few guys calling in sick once the teams have headed off, and we come up short."

He could read Tina's emotions clearly on her face. She looked sad but resigned.

"That's okay, Conner. I understand you have a job to do. I've really appreciated all the time you've spent with me these last few days."

Conner set her in the shower chair gently. He kissed her softly before he set about cleaning them both. He was really going to miss her tonight.

Finally. She'd found the document. Robyn hadn't thought she'd need to use the Medical Power of Attorney so she'd put it away. Frustratingly, she hadn't been able to remember where she'd stored the damn thing. Closing the drawer on the filing cabinet in her salon's office, she went to her bag and put the document inside. She was locking the back door when her phone rang. She looked at the screen, and her whole being tensed. Dale.

"Hello, Dale. What can I do for you?"

"You can start by explaining why you've been preventing Tina from having a social life. She's an adult, Robyn. She is allowed to go on dates and have freedom."

Robyn unlocked and slid into her car before she responded. Damn it, someone had told Dale about Conner. Clenching her free hand around the steering wheel tightly, she went into damage control.

"I was protecting her. She's so vulnerable in the chair. I didn't want some boy taking advantage of her." She lied smoothly, sure her tone indicated no hint of dishonesty.

"Conner White is a good man, Robyn. We went to school with his father. You know that no child of Jake's would be anything other than honorable. You're hiding some other reason."

The anger in Dale's voice brought an ache to her chest. How could she turn this around?

"Conner just feels sorry for her, he'll break her heart. He's been brainwashing her for weeks. I've tried to protect her from him, save her from his mind games."

Dale's sharp voice cut her short. "Stop lying! I'm so tired of your lies. I never should have left Tina in your care. I never thought you'd have been so cruel as to treat her like this. I'll be back in Rosebery early tomorrow morning. Make sure you and all your things are out of my house. I'll have Jake send Conner over to take care of Tina if she gets out of the hospital before I'm back."

Panic rose inside her, boiling up until it consumed her.

"No. I belong in that house. With you-"

"Do you hear yourself? Hear how crazy that sounds? That house is mine and Tina's. We're the only ones who belong there. And you and me? That has never, nor will it ever, happen. I've never felt like that about you."

"I. Am. Not. Crazy."

Her grip on her phone tightened until she heard a crack and the call ended. Stunned, she pulled it from her ear. The phone now sported a large crack across its dark screen. She tried desperately to turn it on but to no avail. Her body began to rock in the seat. She shook her head. "He didn't mean it. We belong together. He needs me."

Part of what he said replayed through her mind, bringing her head up and sharpening her focus.

"I have to get Tina out of the hospital and back to the house before he calls Conner in."

With renewed purpose now she had a goal. She headed over to the hospital. It didn't take long in the midweek evening traffic for her to get there. With her ammo—aka Medical Power of Attorney—fisted in her grip, she stormed into the cream brick building and straight to the office of the head of the hospital. Dr Maynard would listen to her. He was a sensible man.

"Dr Maynard, I found the document I spoke to you about earlier."

She smiled sweetly as his surprised face turned up from his desk toward her. "Robyn, I didn't hear you come in. What document would that be?"

"You know exactly the document I'm referring to."

She paused to place the legal document in front of him. "Signed and legal, it gives me full say in Tina's medical treatment," she allowed him a moment to look over the papers, "and I elect to take Tina home. Now."

Dr Maynard gave her a serious stare. She held his gaze, making sure to not flinch at all. Her insides were churning, her plan ended once she got Tina home. Then what would she do? But she pushed the rising panic down. If the good doctor here saw any of that, he'd never release Tina.

"Okay. We were planning on releasing Tina in the morning, you sure you can't come back then? Give her one more night with medical supervision."

"I'm sure, Doctor. I'll be with her twenty-four/seven to make sure she's recovering well."

He sighed and rubbed the bridge of his nose.

"I'll need to fill out the paperwork. If you would go out to the waiting room, I'll get everything sorted."

With a grin, she thanked the doctor and headed back out to the waiting room where she sat and flipped through a magazine to pass the time. Her smile faded as the minutes crept by. What was she going to do once she got Tina home? She needed to prove that Conner was up to no good, had to prove she'd been protecting Tina all this time. Maybe if Tina told her dad Robyn had been doing a good job...but how to get her to do that...

Someone clearing her throat brought her from her inner thoughts. She tossed down the magazine she'd been holding and strode over to the nurse who stood in the doorway with a clipboard.

"Here are the discharge papers for Tina Anderson. Please sign where indicated."

Robyn barely scanned the pages before signing them. "Done."

"If you'd like to bring your car around to the doors, we'll bring Tina out for you. A nurse is just helping her get dressed."

"A nurse? Conner isn't here?"

A wave of relief swept through her. She didn't want to have to deal with trying to separate Tina from Conner, or that redhead who was here earlier. Robyn was sure if Kit was here, she'd already be out here giving her hell.

"Not just at the moment, I believe he had to work tonight."

"How convenient. I'll go and get my car."

Pulling her keys free of her pocket, she couldn't believe her luck. She'd have hours before Conner would show up. Surely she could suitably scare Tina into helping her with Dale by then.

Conner was helping Nick roll up the hoses and check over the truck. They'd just returned from a small grass fire and were going through all the normal checks when Dominic came barreling into the garage from his office.

"Conner, you gotta get your ass over to the hospital. Like, yesterday."

The hairs on the back of Conner's neck rose.

"Why? What's happened?"

Nick took the hose from his hands and Conner jogged over to his brother.

"Robyn's lost the damn plot. Dale rung her, told her to get out of the house and that he'd get Dad to send you over to watch Tina if she was released from hospital before Dale flies in tomorrow."

"What has she done?"

"We don't know, but Dale told Dad she was talking crazy before the phone cut out. He tried to call her back but it was turned off. Dale thinks she's smashed her phone in a rage. He's really worried Tina's in danger. You need to get over to there to keep her protected. As soon as my shift finishes, I'll head over to back you up."

Dom slapped Conner's shoulder as he sprinted toward the locker room. He didn't stop to change, just grabbed his keys and phone then ran to his car. He drove to the hospital in record time then sprinted into the entrance and headed to Tina's room, Clint's sharp yell drew his attention.

"Conner, wait!"

"What is it, Doc? Make it quick, I gotta get to Tina."

"That's what I want to talk to you about, she's gone."

Conner spun on the other man, "What? How could you let that bitch take her?"

Clint's hands rose in a gesture of peace. "I had no choice, Conner. You know I wouldn't have released her to Robyn if I could have avoided it. Legal documents can't be easily argued with."

"How long ago did they leave?"

"About an hour ago."

Conner didn't hang around to hear anything else. He sprinted out to his car and headed to Tina's house, fighting the urge to shift the whole way as he pondered what the hell Robyn had done to his mate in the past hour.

He pulled up across the road and killed the engine. He sat and watched the house for a minute. How was he going to do this? He couldn't just go knock on the door and demand Robyn leave, especially if she had completely lost the plot.

His instincts went off and his nostrils flared. Smoke. The slightest hint of it was in the air. He wrenched open the door and inhaled deeply. Definitely smoke. He grabbed his mobile out and rang the station.

"Rosebery fire station."

Joel. Great, he was always quick off the mark and didn't muck around with small talk.

"Hey Joel, Conner here. I'm outside Tina's place on Pitt Drive and I smell smoke. You haven't got any reports since I left have you?"

"No, nothing's come through."

A loud whoosh filled the air and he all but dropped his phone when the window of the front bedroom shattered and flames licked out into the night air. Within seconds he could see fire through the glass of the front door. Shit.

Running around the side of the house to the back, he yelled down the phone line to Joel, "Get everyone out here now. Tina's house just went up. Pitt Drive. Front window just blew out, looks like the front rooms are alight. I'm going in the back."

"Conner, don't be a fool, man. Wait for backup. You know better than to run into a burning house on your own!"

"Tina's in there and what's the bet that bitch has taken her chair. I can't not go. See you on the other side, Joel."

He ended the call and slipped the phone back in his pants pocket as he reached the rear of the house, grateful he hadn't changed out of his turnout gear. Putting all his strength behind it, he kicked in the back door, not bothering to waste time checking if it was unlocked. Following her scent, he raced toward Tina. A loud crash sounded as he skidded to a stop in front of Tina's bedroom. With smoke stinging his eyes, he opened the door. "Tina! It's me, Conner. Where are you baby?"

He caught a small sob from over near the window and turned to see that she'd crawled over to the small glass panel. His brave girl was trying to save herself. Another whoosh sounded and a flash of intense heat blasted him from through the doorway. He stripped out of his turnout coat as he ran to her. He quickly got her dressed in it before he scooped her up.

"I'm going to have to sling you over my shoulder. It's the easiest way for me to carry you and run out of here. Keep your head down, shut your eyes and hold your breath. I'll get us out of here."

She gave him a sharp nod and he quickly maneuvered her over his shoulder in a fireman's carry. He turned back toward the doorway—wishing her window wasn't so damn small. He took a deep breath, gripped her legs tightly and stepped through into the hallway. Flames blocked the front door so he quickly spun toward the rear of the house and bolted as fast as he could to get the hell out of there.

He was steps from the rear door when another loud crash sounded. Searing pain radiated through his left shoulder as he was knocked to the side. He fell to his knees, dropping Tina as she screamed for him. He shoved hard at the burning roof beam that had him pinned against the wall, his supernatural strength allowing him to get free. In seconds he had his arm hooked around Tina's waist, hauling her up under his arm as he strode out free of the burning house. The sound of sirens filled the air and Conner had never been so thankful.

He stumbled out to the swing and lowered Tina as gently as he could to the grass moments before his knees buckled and he crumpled to the ground with a growl of frustration. He shook his head as black spots swam before his vision. Agony radiated from his shoulder and bicep but he focused on Tina. She was dragging herself over to him, her full attention on his left arm. Her pain filled gaze flicked to his.

"Oh, baby, your arm. You need to lie down until the ambulance gets here. You're looking really pale."

Leaning on his right arm he moved so his head was resting on Tina's tummy.

"I didn't hurt you? I'm sorry I dropped you."

"I'm fine, and you were knocked over by a burning hunk of wood. Dropping me isn't your fault. You saved me. I would have burned to death if it weren't for you."

"Where's Robyn? Did she do this on purpose?"

"I don't know where she is. I heard her scream and run for the back of the house just as I smelled smoke."

Conner couldn't help but growl. "She left you to burn? On purpose!"

"But you saved me. It's okay. I'm safe now. Shhh."

He nuzzled his face into her soft tummy, and relaxed into her as she stroked his face and hair. Without his consent, his eyes drifted shut. He inhaled Tina's citrusy scent as he floated away from the pain into darkness.

Chapter Eight

Briefly releasing Conner's hand, Tina swiped a tear from her cheek. His color looked better but he hadn't woken up yet. He'd passed out with his head resting on her tummy. She'd never felt so frustrated at her lack of movement as she had in that moment. She could do nothing for him. Waiting for the ambulance and fire trucks to arrive she stroked his hair and face, but couldn't pull her stare from the horrific charred flesh on his shoulder and arm. Injuries he'd received rescuing her. If only he hadn't given her his thick protective coat. The one she still wore. Burying her nose in the heavy yellow material, she breathed deeply of Conner's scent mixed with smoke. It made her feel like he was embracing her.

"Please don't cry. Your tears break my heart."

She closed her eyes briefly before looking over at Conner in relief. He was awake. He was going to be okay.

"You're finally back with us. You've had me so worried."

He frowned for a moment. "How long have I been out?"

Tina glanced at the clock high on the hospital

room's wall. "Not really sure, I didn't look at the time when we came in. But it was more than three hours ago when we arrived."

She lifted his hand and kissed his palm. She'd have loved to climb on the bed with him, but couldn't. *Damn my useless leg!* His thumb stroked her face, his calloused skin feeling so good against her soft cheek.

He gently chuckled. "Got myself my very own Cinderella."

She frowned up at him. "How so?"

"You're covered in soot and ash, like you would if you'd been sleeping in a fireplace. And Robyn's been keeping you locked up and making you work, just like Cinderella."

She shook her head on a giggle. "Well, that's only fair since you're my knight in shining armor that keeps coming in to rescue me—gotta do the damsel in distress thing properly you know?"

"So I'm not Prince Charming? Just a run of the mill knight, huh?"

Tina smiled at her cheeky man. Only Conner could turn her tears to laughter so quickly.

"You're pretty charming when you put your mind to it. I just liked the image of you riding in on a big stallion to rescue me in your armor better than the pretty boy, useless male that Prince Charming usually is."

"Well, when you put it like that, I'll stay with being your knight."

Suddenly his face lost all humor, his serious gaze

holding hers captive.

"I love you, Tina. I'll come running to your rescue no matter how many times I have to. I'd do anything to keep you safe."

Tina's breath froze in her chest as her heart began to beat wildly. Over the course of the past day she'd come to the conclusion she loved him too, but could she tell him? Could she open herself up to him like that? He made to move his hand toward her, obviously forgetting about his burns. As she watched him wince and lower his hand again, she knew her answer. After all, he'd run through a burning house for her.

"I love you too, Conner. Any time you're near, I feel safe. When you came into my room earlier, I've never seen a more beautiful sight. I was sure I was going to die in that house."

Tears blurred her vision and Conner groaned. "Damn, I wish I could hold you right now."

"Well, little brother. Let me check that shoulder and I'll help get Tina up to you."

Adele's sweet voice floated through the room and Tina quickly dashed the tears from her eyes as Adele approached the bed and leaned in to kiss Conner's cheek.

"Gave us all quite a scare earlier. No more running into burning houses alone before back -up comes, you hear me?"

"Sorry about scaring everyone, but I can't promise you I won't do it again. I'd run into a thousand burning houses alone if that's what was needed to keep my Tina safe."

Tina's heart swelled. How had she managed to score such a noble man?

With a small shake of her head, Adele began peeling the tape from the bandage on his shoulder.

"Isn't it too soon? Surely the burn would still be raw?"

"She knows what you are, doesn't she Conner?"

"Yeah, she knows about us."

"Tina, shifters heal at a very rapid rate. Conner's skin should be scar tissue at this point. The pain will last a while longer. If he was human, he would have broken at least one bone, I'm sure. Even though nothing broke, he got banged around pretty good. His shoulder and arm are going to ache for probably two or three days."

Tina watched transfixed as Adele peeled the bandage from Conner's skin. As the edge of the wound was revealed Tina jerked in her chair.

"What the hell?"

"I have no idea. I'm pretty new to this shifter thing myself. Conner, care to explain your funky scar?"

Conner looked down at his arm with a small grin. "Cheaper than getting a tattoo."

She watched as Adele's finger slid over the scar tissue, which looked like several leopard spots.

"When a shifter's skin is burned, our spots show though the scar. For some reason, it only happens with burns. Any other wound heals as a human's would."

"Wow. Well, they say you should learn a new

thing every day. How does it feel, Conner? Any tightness? Pain?"

"Nah, it's good. Just a little achy in the bones and joints like you said before."

"Okay, well, we'll leave the bandages off then. I'll help Tina up on the bed then go fill out your paperwork. You can leave as soon as I'm done."

"Can you please call Dad or Dom to come pick us up too?"

"Sure thing, Conner."

"Thanks, sis."

Tina let Adele help her up onto the bed. For such a small woman, she was surprisingly strong.

"Adele, are you a shifter too?"

"Sure am. I've only been one for a little while though. That story can wait for another time. I'll leave you two alone for a bit while I get everything sorted for your discharge."

Conner wrapped his arms around her and pulled her over his chest. She snuggled into the indent of his shoulder and inhaled against his skin, allowing his scent to fill her senses. Then reality came crashing down.

"I have no home."

A sob wrenched from her body as the realization hit her of what the fire had taken.

"Shh, baby doll, you can stay with me. Mum will love having another woman around the place. And we can go check the house. I'm not sure how long it burned, but hopefully some of your things survived."

He stroked her hair and back as he laid a reverent kiss on her forehead. Soon her tears eased and she turned her face to look over at his burned arm. She raised her fingertip and traced his new spots in awe.

"Does it hurt?"

"Not at all. It's deep down that still aches a little. I'll be right as rain in no time, you just wait and see." He paused to give her another light kiss. "Close your eyes for a bit, Tina. Rest. I'll have you home and cleaned up soon. Then we can both curl up in a bigger bed and get some serious sleep."

With a smile, she snuggled into his warmth. She really liked the sound of that plan.

Scrubbing his face with his hand, Dale watched the carousel begin to bring the luggage around from his flight. With a heavy heart, he waited for his bag. How had he failed his daughter so badly? Robyn hadn't provided her with any care. All she'd done was add to Tina's torment. At least the hospital psychiatrist, Dr Reid, had sounded nice. She'd told him she was more than happy to work with him and Tina to help her recover her inner strength. He'd spoken to Dr Reid yesterday and she was going to see him and Tina later today.

"Dale, long time no see."

He turned to face a man he hadn't seen in a very long time. "Jake?"

"That's me. How was the flight?"

"Fine, just a day later than I wanted it to be.

What's going on?"

"More than you know, buddy."

Dale frowned at Jake, "What do you mean? What's happened since we spoke last?"

"Let's grab your bags and I'll explain in the car. You're not going to want to be in a public place when I tell you."

With his heart in his throat, he licked his dry lips. "Is Tina okay?"

"She's safe now."

Now. That implied earlier she wasn't. Could this situation get any worse? He turned back to the carousel and spotted his large bag coming toward him. He quickly snagged it from the belt.

"Let's get moving then."

Dale followed Jake out toward the car park. Launceston Airport was a small operation and it didn't take more than ten minutes to get to the car. As he heard Jake turn the key in the ignition, he felt Jake's gaze bore into him.

"When did you last speak with Robyn?"

"I rang her early last night, just before I rang you and told you how she'd gone crazy. Her phone hasn't been switched on since then. I've tried it a couple times. You told me Tina was still in hospital and wasn't going to be released until this morning. What happened?"

"Okay, well, obviously your call set her off worse than you suspected. She took that damn Medical Power of Attorney of hers around to the hospital and got Dr

Maynard to release Tina into her care. Trust me, Clint didn't want to, but he had no choice."

"What the hell have I done?" He scrubbed at his face as he spoke, his beard scratching his palms.

"You did what you had to, Dale. Don't beat yourself up over this. Robyn has made her own choices. You couldn't have known how close to the edge she was."

Dale dreaded finding out what had happened, but he couldn't put it off. He needed to know.

"Please, Jake, just tell me what happened last night."

"After our call, I rang my boys and Conner went to the hospital. But Robyn had already taken Tina. He went straight to your place and arrived in the nick of time to get Tina out of the place before it was engulfed in flames."

Bile rose in Dale's throat as his lungs froze up. "She set the house on fire? With my baby girl inside!" He could hear the growl in his voice but didn't care. How could anyone do such a thing?

"We don't know what happened. So far, all we know is that the fire started in the master bedroom where Robyn was staying. Tina heard her run out the back door as she smelled the smoke. Robyn had taken her chair so Tina made her way to the window to try and escape. That's how Conner found her. He got her out. Just. A burning roof beam slammed into him injuring his shoulder and caused him to drop her. She was wearing his turnout coat, so hasn't got more than a few bruises, and my boy heals real quick. He'll be a little slower than usual for a bit, but thankfully that's all."

Again, he scrubbed his face with both his palms, feeling moisture on them from his eyes.

"On the phone, Robyn said she belonged in the house, with me. She was meant to be staying in the spare room, not my bloody bedroom. I think she has some delusion I'm in love with her. She always followed Gloria around back in school. Drove me nuts when I was trying to get alone time with Gloria, Robyn was always there. How could I have been so stupid? Not seen what she was up to..."

"You couldn't have known. No one knew what she was playing at. Well, maybe Barbara at the salon might have had a clue."

"Where's Robyn now?"

He wasn't sure if he wanted to know the answer, but he'd spoken the words now.

"No one knows. The police are looking for her. Her house looks quiet and locked up tight. There's a patrol car sitting out front waiting for her if she does go there."

"And Tina?"

"She refused to leave Conner while he was in the hospital. He was released late last night and they headed back to my place after that."

"Just...take me to my daughter. Please, Jake, I need to see her."

"That's the plan. We still have a little over an hour of driving to go. Why don't you try to get some shuteye while you can? You've got a busy couple of days coming up."

"Yeah, sure do."

"You and Tina can stay with us, by the way. We've got plenty of room."

"Thanks, mate."

Dale let his lids shut as horrific images of his sweet pea being trapped in a fire played through his mind. If he ever got his hands on Robyn, he'd be sorely tempted to strangle the life out of the damn woman.

Tina woke to find herself in a strange bed. Attempting to roll over, she pressed against a warm wall of muscle. Conner. The previous night came back to her. After Conner had been released from the hospital, Dominic had driven them back to where Conner lived with his parents. After she protested that Conner shouldn't be lifting her with his shoulder, Dominic carried her inside while Conner grumbled and muttered the whole way about it being his job. After a quick introduction to Jake and Sophie, she'd been carried down to the far end of the house and laid on a large soft bed. Dominic had kissed her cheek, bid her good night and left. Conner growled at his brother the entire time, which just made Dominic chuckle.

As soon as the way was clear, he'd firmly closed the door. Her body heated instantly as he turned to prowl over to the bed. In a very feline manner, he'd climbed onto the end of the bed and crawled up over her body.

"I have never been as scared as I was today, baby doll. When I got word that Robyn had you, that she'd had you for an hour..."

He'd shuddered above her. His eyes squeezed shut and she saw a look of agony pass over his face. She'd reached up, took his face between her hands and pulled him down to her lips. With a groan, he'd taken over control and devoured her mouth with his.

An arm tightening around her waist pulled her mind back to the now. She wriggled her hips a little and enjoyed the low growl he made as his hard shaft rubbed against her ass.

"Morning, baby doll."

His hand slid up her naked abdomen toward her breasts, and he cupped one and ran his thumb back and forth over the peak. Her breath caught as her nipple hardened beneath his tender caress.

"I could definitely get used to this."

"What's that?" Her voice hitched as he continued to tease her nipple.

"Waking up to you in my arms. Going to sleep with you here in my bed with me."

A smile crept over her face and she snuggled back into his chest. "Me too. I feel safe and protected when you're near, but especially when I'm wrapped in your arms."

"That's because you are. I'll always do

everything I can to keep you from harm."

"I know you will. I just hope it's enough. She's really crazy."

A low growl filled the air before she felt Conner nip her earlobe. "No talk of that bitch in our bed."

He rolled her on to her back and covered her body with his, her hands raising instinctively to his solid chest. One hand trailed up to his shoulder where she traced his spots with her fingers. They really did look like tattoos. A soft purr filled the air moments before Conner lowered to her neck to nuzzle against her skin.

"Hmm, Conner... But what about your parents?"

"Their room is at the other end of the house, but they've both left already. They had things to do early this morning. We've got the whole place to ourselves, baby."

He licked up her neck and nibbled along her jaw. After kissing her senseless, he moved down to her breasts. His muscular abdomen nestled into the cradle of her body as he settled in to lavish her flesh with attention. He licked, nipped and sucked until she was pulling at his hair as she writhed beneath him.

With a small chuckle, he moved down, kissing his way over her tummy and further down. Just like last time, he gently lifted her right leg as she moved her left.

"You are so beautiful, Tina."

His softly spoken words made her shiver until he pressed his tongue against her damp heat. With one stroke, her mind went blank. Pure pleasure flowed through and over her as Conner lavished attention on her sensitive flesh. She could feel the heat coiling in her lower belly, tighter and tighter until she was arching off the bed. With her fingers fisted in the bed sheet, she cried out as she came apart for him.

Still floating back to herself, she felt Conner slide his latex covered length into her as his mouth took hers with a gentle passion. His strokes were slow and deliberate. Each glide he made touched her inner bundle of nerves. Before Conner, she'd been convinced the concept of a G-spot had been made up. Not anymore, Conner aimed for it as if he'd had a map to its location from the beginning.

Conner kept her body on a simmer as he gently made love to her, his tenderness cracking her heart wide open. He feathered kisses over her cheek, up to her ear, where he started whispering sweet nothings to her. His words of adoration and protection caused Tina's eyes to tear up. Unsure she was deserving of this amazing man's affection and love, she suddenly felt awkward beneath him. Could she love him back at the level he deserved?

He must have registered her change in mood, as he pulled back before kissing away her tears.

"Don't cry, love. I've got you."

She was thankful when his strokes increased in speed, tightening the coil of arousal yet again. Her mind cleared of everything but the pleasure he was giving her.

"Faster, Conner. I need you."

With a groan, he did as she asked. She dug her nails into his shoulders as she tilted her hips toward him.

He gripped her right leg and moved it up onto his shoulder, opening her up without moving her injured left leg. Holding his weight on his outstretched arms, he began pounding into her, reaching even deeper inside her. Tina moved with him, encouraging him into her warmth. With her desire fogged gaze, she watched beads of sweat run down his face. He was so damn sexy. Moments before her body climaxed, his passion-soaked gaze caught hers and he held himself still within her as she felt him pulse within her tightening muscles.

"I will never get enough of making love to you."

With her heart already cracked open, Conner's declaration brought all her emotions to the surface. Conner lowered her leg back down and she clung to his sweaty body as she sobbed for all she'd endured in the past months.

"Shh, I'm sorry, baby doll. I didn't mean to upset you. Did I hurt you?"

"You didn't. You're perfect. Too perfect, I'm not sure I deserve you."

"Oh, baby. I'm nowhere near perfect, but you do deserve perfection. You are just right for me. No one else could ever complete me the way you do. No. One."

"I'm sorry, I didn't mean to ruin our moment."

"You didn't ruin it, Tina. Making love to you was incredible. Already, I can't wait until I can get you alone next so we can do it all over again."

A watery sounding giggle escaped Tina. "You're shocking."

He nibbled at her jaw. "Only for you. Join me for a shower?"

Sadness swamped her. She didn't want to face the day. The cold reality of her life. She wanted to stay here, warm and safe in Conner's embrace.

"Do we have to get up?"

He playfully nipped at the tip of her nose. "Yes, we do. I don't want to meet your dad for the first time naked and sweaty, lying on top of his daughter."

Her breath hitched, "Dad? He's coming here? Dr Reid told me he was going to try to leave his job and come back, but with Robyn taking my phone I couldn't ring him myself."

"My dad went to collect him from the Launceston airport. They should be here before too long."

Panic washed through her excitement. "I don't have any clothes, or my wheelchair. Or my shower chair." Tears filled her eyes again as she realized the extent of all she'd lost in the fire.

"It's all sorted, baby doll. Adele dropped off a chair from the hospital for you to use until we can get you a new one. I am more than happy to help you wash this totally delectable body each day. And you can wear one of my shirts and I'll grab a pair of pants from Mum. I'll take you shopping later for new clothes."

"You have a solution for everything, don't you?"

"Not quite, sweetheart."

He gave her the most reverent kiss she'd ever received before he rose from the bed. She watched him dispose of the condom in a tissue that he tossed into the bin before he returned to scoop her up and head toward the en-suite bathroom.

With a newfound sense of contentment Conner carried Tina into the kitchen. He knew she was frustrated at not being able to walk herself, but he rather liked carrying her in his arms. He gently settled her onto a chair at the table with a kiss on her temple.

"What would you like for breakfast, baby doll?"

He watched as she nervously pushed her thick blond hair behind her ear, itching to do it for her. He wanted to slide his fingers through the silky strands, but the slight blush on her cheeks stopped him.

"What's this for?"

He brushed his thumb over her smooth, reddened skin.

"It's nothing. I'm just, not used to being carried around. I was always independent, even when I was living with my mother. Now, I can't even get myself breakfast."

"You know, I was just thinking how convenient it was that I *had* to carry you around the place. Because, Tina, I love having you in my arms, taking care of you."

She frowned before she glared at him. "My being a cripple is *convenient* to you?"

Oh crap, Conner's breath froze as he realized she'd taken what he'd said completely the wrong way. Conner wished he was more eloquent with words. He wasn't sure how he could make her understand.

He dropped to his knees and took her face between his palms, "Tina, you are not a cripple. This is temporary. I'll work with you on your rehab and you'll get back your full mobility. I'm sorry if I offended you, baby. I'm not real good with explaining myself most days. I meant that being able to carry you more often is convenient, not your injury. It tears at my soul that you've been injured so severely."

The single tear that slid down her cheek cracked his heart open.

"I'm sorry, Conner. I'm just feeling on edge. I didn't mean to lash out at you. So much has happened in such a short period of time. My head is spinning from it all."

He leaned in to give her a tender kiss, "I know, baby doll. How about we start with breakfast? Bacon and eggs? Cereal? Toast? Coffee?"

Her hand came up and he reveled in the feel of her fingers softly caressing his face. "Toast and a coffee would be great. Thank you, Conner. For everything."

"It's no trouble, sweetheart. I love you and would do anything for you."

She pressed her lips against his and gave him a gentle but ever so powerful kiss. "I love you too, Conner."

With a groan, he forced himself to leave her to get their breakfast on the go. He'd happily spend all day lavishing attention on his mate, but their fathers would be arriving soon.

He placed bread in the toaster and poured himself a bowl of cereal. He didn't have time to muck about with eggs and bacon.

"How do you have your coffee?"

"White with one."

"Same as me."

He set about making the coffees and in no time both of them were munching away on their breakfast and drinking their java. Conner enjoyed watching Tina eat. All her movements were smooth and graceful, her gymnastics training evident in each gesture she made.

As they were both finishing off, Conner heard a car pull up. Pushing his chair back, he quickly retrieved the loaner wheelchair from the lounge room. He was pretty sure Tina would want to meet her dad under her own steam. Wheeling it into the kitchen, his heart stopped as he watched Tina trying to get up from the chair on her own. He raced to her, wrapping his arm around her waist as she staggered.

"What are you doing? You could fall, injure yourself again."

"I thought I heard a car. Is it my dad?"

"Yeah, baby doll. It's our dads."

With fear for her still coursing through his body, he scooped her up and deposited her into the chair. He gave her a kiss on the top of her head, lingering to inhale her scent for a moment, allowing her natural citrus fragrance to calm him, before allowing her to wheel herself toward the front door.

"I'm going to need a new pair of gloves. My skin is still too soft, and it aches from pushing the wheels without the extra padding."

"Let me push you then. I'll take you shopping today, Tina. We'll get everything you need then, okay?"

"Yeah, that would be great. You don't have to work?"

"Only if there's a major callout. They're still a little short staffed, but so long as no big fires flare up they should be right without me."

He saw her tense as the front door swung open and his dad came in.

"Here she is, Dale. Waiting for you."

His dad came over, laid a kiss on Tina's head before giving Conner a quick hug.

"Hey, Dad, uneventful drive over?"

"Yeah, clear roads the whole way. Made great time."

Conner turned from his father to the doorway. Dale looked wrecked, but then again, a few days in airports and on planes could do that to a person.

"Sweet pea..."

Conner's heart stuttered as Dale knelt before his daughter and embraced her in the chair. Tina's sobs as she clung to her father had him blinking back his own tears. Damn, this woman was going to be the end of him. His dad's hand on his shoulder brought his attention away from emotional reunion.

"C'mon, son. Let's give them a minute or two."

With a nod, Conner allowed his dad to steer him back toward the kitchen.

Chapter Nine

Holding his precious daughter tightly, Dale breathed deeply for the first time in days, finally allowing himself to believe she was unharmed and safe. He kept her in his embrace as she cried.

"I am so sorry, Tina."

Through her slowing tears, Tina spoke, "It's not your fault, Dad. You couldn't have known how crazy she was."

No, but he could have checked her out a little more. Could have hired a trained nurse. He knew he'd be living with his regrets for a long time, no matter how swiftly his daughter forgave him.

"Why didn't you ever tell me how bad she was, sweet pea?"

"I don't know. I knew she'd get worse if you knew what she was doing, and you wouldn't have been able to get back to me quickly. Honestly, there wasn't any one thing that she did that was bad in itself that I could have told you about. Well, aside from the no rehab thing. When you first left, my focus was on the chaos in my mind. I didn't really notice what she was doing. I didn't notice how far I'd slipped until Conner." She paused and took a deep breath. "I met Conner at the salon. He was picking up his mum, his brother's bride-to-be and her daughter. I was heading to the counter to grab the receipts to enter in-"

"You were doing what?"

Damn it, Dale's blood began heating. He paid Robyn well to look after Tina. There was certainly no need for Robyn to put Tina to work! He bet his last dollar Robyn didn't pay her either.

"Robyn worked out pretty quickly that I was good with numbers. So she made me do all of the salon's bookwork. It wasn't a big deal, Dad. It actually gave me something to do."

"It is a big deal. She forced you to work for her, and I can put money on her not paying you for all your hard work."

"Ha, yeah, your money's safe on that bet. *Anyway*, Conner ran into my chair, when I crossed in front of the door as he came in. Robyn obviously saw that we were interested in one another because she wheeled me away quick smart, and herded Conner and his family out pretty fast too.

"Conner came back a few times after that. I saw him. Heard the foul things Robyn said to him and accused him of. Anyway, that kind of clued me in on things I'd been ignoring. I started watching her a little more closely. You know she was sleeping in your room? Not the spare one, like you told her to."

Even though Jake had told him part of this story, he

didn't want to stop Tina from telling her version of things, so he didn't let on what Jake had told him on the drive over.

"She was doing what? I told her that was a hard and fast rule. My room was off limits."

Man, maybe the fact his house had burned wasn't so bad. He couldn't handle sleeping where that nutcase had laid her head.

"Conner and I started meeting at the swing at night, after Robyn had gone to bed, but she found out after a couple weeks. That's when she took my phone and started taking my chair at night. I wanted to ring you but I couldn't get my phone and I didn't know if you'd be able to answer out on the rig."

"Oh, sweet pea. No wonder you weren't answering my calls. I'm just so sorry. Can you ever forgive me for doing this to you?"

She gave him a sweet kiss on his cheek, "Dad, there's nothing to forgive. You did what you had to. I'm an adult. I do understand how the world works, you know?"

"That you do. Probably better than you should have to."

"I understand Robyn better now too. In the last month I've started paying more attention. Robyn tells Barbara—her employee at the salon—everything. There's no door to the back room, just a curtain. I heard a lot of what they spoke about."

"I'm pretty sure I know where you're going with this, but please, tell me what you picked up."

"She's madly in love with you, Dad. Has been since high school. She was and still is insanely jealous of my mother. She said she only tolerated being friends with her so she could be near you. She said more than once that taking on my care was just a means to an end. Apparently, you were meant to fall at her feet in gratitude, completely in love with her."

A humorless laugh left his throat. "You got the madly and insanely parts right. I barely noticed her. She was Gloria's shadow. I never thought of her as anything more."

Tina's next words, spoken quietly, were filled with so much pain it ripped through him all the way to his core. "The house is gone, Dad. I couldn't grab anything."

"It's all just stuff, sweet pea. We can replace all that. Just so long as *you* got out, that's all that matters. How about we go over in a bit and see if we can salvage anything? You never know our luck."

"Sounds good, Dad. Conner can come too, right?"

"Want to tell your old man what's going on between you two?"

"He makes me so happy, Dad. I'm in love for the first time, and he loves me."

"Just take it slow, Tina. Don't rush into anything."

Her short laugh made his chest tighten with worry. She brought her hand up to show him a beautiful elegant emerald and diamond ring. Shit, it was on her left ring finger.

"He proposed? Already?"

Maybe Robyn had a point with Conner.

Tina opened her mouth but before a sound came out, Conner's voice came from the doorway. "Sorry, Mr Anderson. I would have asked your permission if I could have gotten hold of you. I love your daughter very much. I want to spend the rest of my life with her by my side. I think I've more than proved my intentions are pure."

"He's saved my life more than once, Dad. I haven't been the easiest person to be around, yet he's still here."

Dale looked from his daughter to Conner; their gazes were now locked and it was perfectly clear the love and affection that flowed between them. Looks like his daughter was getting hitched in the near future. He sighed as he scrubbed his face with his hands.

"I guess, so long as you both are happy and committed to make it last forever, I'm good."

They both quickly assured him it was definitely forever.

Unable to contemplate his little girl getting married, he decided a change of subject was in order. "How about we go check out what's left of our house? Then Tina and I have an appointment with Dr Reid at the hospital."

After accepting a travel mug of coffee from Jake, he followed Conner and Tina out of the house to go see how much of his was left. Something he really wasn't looking forward to doing, but something that had to be done.

Robyn flexed her hands in frustration, feeling the burned skin tighten and bite. She forced her fingers to relax then examined them closely and noticed more than one blister had burst. The throbbing pain and heat radiating from her burns was intense, but she couldn't go to the hospital. They'd lock her up.

"I need to get to Dale, explain what happened."

Then he could tell the police they didn't need to charge her. Dale could fix it all. Then she'd go to the hospital.

She shifted her position as a car pulled up across the road. She shuffled forward from where she knelt hidden behind some shrubs, twigs and rocks roughening up her legs. They'd only been slightly singed by the flames but they still didn't appreciate the scuffing up.

She watched as a forest green Prado pulled up in front of the charred house. Her gaze followed Conner as he got out and retrieved a crappy old wheelchair from the rear.

"Damn it! I don't need Tina. I only need Dale."

As if her thoughts had called him, he stepped free from the vehicle and helped Conner get Tina from the car and into her chair before they headed into the remains of the house. Even though the firefighters had arrived quickly last night, the house was basically gutted. It was really bad, but not entirely gone. The roof had completely caved in so she'd guess no one would be allowed into the actual house before an inspector of some sort okayed it.

She sat back, making sure she was still hidden from view, and watched as the three of them moved around the ruined structure. Conner carefully slipped into the building a few times, returning with little bits of stuff which he handed to Tina or Dale. She was pretty sure the fire inspector would have something to say about them messing with the scene, but she really didn't care. In fact, maybe if they compromised the scene, she'd get away with it.

Not that it had been intentional.

Far from it.

She'd been innocently sitting cross-legged on Dale's bed, nursing a candle, which she moved from hand to hand slowly as she focused on the flicker at the tip of the wick. Watching a flame had always soothed her. But her hand had twitched unexpectedly and she'd dropped the candle, the flame quickly igniting the quilt cover. Stupidly, she'd attempted to smother the fire with her hands. Dumb move, but in the heat of the moment she didn't think. As she cried out in pain, the flames took flight over the bed and on to the floor, quickly engulfing the curtains. She'd rushed from the room as fast as she could and singed her legs through the thick denim jeans she had on as she'd crawled from the burning mattress. In her panic she'd fled the house, not remembering Tina at all until she was well away from the fire. She'd come back to see if she'd gotten out. Dale would never forgive her if Tina had died, or been harmed in the fire. She'd been trying to work out a way to get into the house when Conner came out with Tina slung under his arm.

"The boy does have some useful qualities," she quietly admitted to herself.

After realizing Tina was safely away, she'd made herself comfortable in the shrub across the road and awaited daybreak. She knew Dale would be coming home soon. She just needed to be patient, wait for him. He'd listen to her. He'd understand it was all an accident. Then, he would be hers.

Robyn turned her attention across the road as they got back into the car. She was just close enough to hear the odd word. She got 'appointment' and 'Reid'. Reid, that was the name of that annoying shrink at the hospital. She pulled herself up and began walking in the direction of the hospital. She could sneak in and approach Dale there. Maybe afterwards she'd get her hands treated properly.

"The perfect plan."

Half an hour later she stood behind some trees near the delivery entrance of the hospital. The walk had worn her out. The pain from her burns combined with her lack of sleep, left her feeling considerably unwell.

"I can't give up now. I've come too far and am too close."

She easily slipped through the door and into a storage room. Glancing around, a box of syringes caught her gaze. She smiled as her mind formed a plan. But before she acted on it, she found the burn kits. She covered her raw flesh with silica cream before she carefully wrapped gauze around her hands. Thankfully, her fingertips had escaped being too badly burned. She gingerly took a wrapped syringe and slipped it up her sleeve for later use. Then taking another, she opened it and pulled the plunger up. A nice shot of air into someone's bloodstream would cause havoc—even if she missed a vein, she was pretty sure her victim would still not want her to push the plunger down.

Satisfied she was now armed appropriately, Robyn made her way toward the consulting rooms where the shrink saw most of her patients. Her heart rate did triple time as she heard footsteps coming down the hallway but she managed to quietly slide into an empty patient room. She held her breath as she heard a squeak of a wheel pass the door along with the heavy footsteps. Oh, how convenient. Conner and Tina had left Dale all by his lonesome. She might not need her syringes after all.

Holding her weapon so it was hidden behind her wrist, she crept from the room and quickly headed down the hallway toward her man.

Dale stood in shocked silence, looking at Jennifer as Conner left with Tina. Dr Reid was Jennifer. The same Jennifer he'd crushed on in school, before he'd met Gloria. In fact, if Jennifer hadn't turned him down, he doubted he would have even given Gloria the time of day. But she'd been Jennifer Wilson back then, which meant she was married. Reid, he knew that name. Dale forced himself to think back to his school days. Ryan Reid, he was a big bloke. Gentle giant that he was, had refused to join the football team. Dale couldn't blame him for chasing after Jennifer. She had been beautiful and very smart. Still was, on both counts.

"So, Dale. How are you coping with everything?"

"Well, I realized I put my daughter in the care of a crazy woman and got a phone call after she attempted suicide. Raced home in time to see my house burned down and to discover my daughter has gotten engaged. It's been a rather busy week."

Jennifer softly chuckled. "And you can throw jetlag in on top of all that too. How about you give yourself a couple of days to reset your body clock to Aussie time? Get rested up, then come back and see me. We'll have a chat about how you're coping with everything then, after you've had some time to process it all."

Yeah, however he doubted a couple days would be long enough for him to process all of it. Especially the fact his old flame was standing before him.

"I can't believe it's you."

She frowned over at him. "What do you mean?"

"When we spoke on the phone, I didn't realize it was you. Jennifer Wilson."

"Well, it's Jennifer Reid now, but yeah, it's me."

"How's Ryan doing these days?"

He frowned as her entire body stiffened. "He died. Accident at the mines several years back now."

"Oh shit, I'm sorry, Jen. Didn't mean to drag up painful memories."

"That's okay, Dale. It happened a long time ago, I've had plenty of time to adjust to being a widow. I'm surprised you remembered either of us, to be honest."

"Seriously? How could I forget my first crush? You

shattered my poor pre-teen heart when you turned down my advances."

She laughed with a smile that reached her eyes. Dale was so glad to see the sad edge to her expression disappear.

"Now that day I remember. You were so sweet. I wanted to give in to your charms, but I knew you weren't meant for me."

He stood from where he'd been leaning against the wall and moved toward her. "So, you found me charming. But how could you have known I wasn't meant for you?"

He was now standing quite close to her, breathing in her feminine scent. She shocked him when she raised a hand and rubbed her thumb over his bearded cheek. "We're a breed apart, Dale. Not that it matters anymore-"

Caught off guard, Dale was slammed into the wall as a high pitch screech rent the air. *What the hell?*

"Get your filthy paws off my man, Jennifer. I lost him once to Gloria. I will not lose him again to you."

Dale pushed himself from the wall. "Damn it, Robyn, what the hell are you going on about?"

"You are mine! We were always meant to be together."

Dale's mind still spun a little from the fast meeting with the wall, but he focused on Robyn's twitching, dilated eyes. Her whole body vibrated with rage.

When had her crush turned so psychotic?

He caught Jennifer's movement out the corner of his

eye. It looked like she'd hit something on the underside of her desktop. A small amount of relief washed through him. She had a panic button. Help was on the way. He just hoped it would be in time.

"Robyn, can you take a couple of deep breaths for me? You need to calm down so we can get a doctor to check you over. You have burns that need care. We can talk about Dale after you get fixed up if you like."

He watched with his heart in his throat as Robyn turned her full focus from him to Jennifer. "There is no need for us to *talk* about Dale. He is mine. No one else's. You hear me?"

The door slammed open and a male nurse ran in, straight in front of Robyn. *Stupid idiot.*

The next minute rolled past like he was watching a movie stuck on slow motion. Robyn grabbed the nurse and brought up a needle she'd been hiding, aimed at the side of his neck. A roar from his right caught his attention and a large snow leopard pounced forward knocking both Robyn and the nurse to the ground. With a loud thump, both were left unconscious, their heads bouncing once on the hard floor. Conner sprinted into the room with Tina wheeling in behind him.

Time sped back up as Tina approached him. "You okay, Dad? You're not hurt?"

He looked back to the large cat now pacing back and forth in the room.

"I'm fine. But there's a leopard- Where's Jennifer?"

His gaze searched the room, finding no sign of her.

His heart rate sped up again, had the leopard injured Jen? Where was she?

"It's okay, Dad. I'll explain it all but you need to calm down first. Here, sit down."

As he sat, Conner's deep voice caught his attention. "Clint, we've got a situation down in Jennifer's office. I need a change of clothes for Jennifer, then we're going to need a couple of stretchers and the police need to be called. Robyn attacked a nurse in the office. Yeah, everyone's okay. The nurse is out cold, as is Robyn. She's also got some nasty looking burns by the look of it. Yep, okay see you in a few. Oh, can you bring a bottle of water. Dale's looking like he's seen better days."

Dale's brain refused to process what he'd seen. It couldn't be possible, could it?

"It's crazy, Dad. I know it is. But it's real. Shape shifters are very real."

Shape shifters? He glared at his daughter, thinking maybe she had lost her mind...but there was a large cat pacing the room with them and no sign of the good doctor.

Clint raced into the room with a pair of sweatpants and a t-shirt. "Sorry, Jen, I know it's not your usual attire but it's all I've got for now." Clint went over to the desk and set the clothing on the corner before he moved to check first the nurse, then Robyn.

The leopard padded behind the desk where a blue bubble engulfed it and the cat shimmered into a female human form. With her back to him, Jennifer dressed quickly before turning around to face him.

"Like I said, Dale. We're just a breed apart."

Dale managed a jerky nod before his brain called it quits. Sorting out the whole damn mess seemed near impossible. Black spots swam before his eyes as he heard Tina call out for someone to grab him.

Tina focused on her father's pale face. Conner had thankfully caught him before he fell from the chair and now he was lying in a hospital bed. He'd had one hell of a day she supposed. She knew how freaked out a person could get when they first discovered shape shifters were not only real, but all around them. The nurse had told her he should wake up soon. He was simply in shock. His small groan had her gripping his hand.

"What happened?"

"Well, Dad, that rather depends on what you remember last?"

Her father rolled his head over and gazed into her eyes. "A snow leopard saved that nurse from Robyn."

"Well, after that you went into shock and passed out. Conner caught you before you fell off the chair, and now here you are."

His eyes narrowed. "What happened to the leopard?"

"Ah, you don't remember that bit. Jennifer is a shifter. She can be either human or snow leopard," she swallowed her rising nerves, "just like Conner can."

Her dad's eyes opened wide before narrowing again. "Your fiancé is part animal?"

"It's not like that, Dad. Get Jake to explain it. I'll forget bits if I do it."

"Wait, Jake's one too? How many are there?"

"I don't know exactly. There's a whole Leap here in Rosebery. That's what a group of leopards is called, a Leap. I thought it was a Pride, but that's lions. Anyway, most of the firefighters are shifters. Obviously Jennifer is one. Not sure who else. But you don't have to worry, Dad. They're protectors, guardians. They won't ever hurt anyone without good cause. Look at Robyn. Jennifer could have killed her, but she just knocked her out."

Her father sat up, swinging his legs over the side of the bed so he was looking down into her face.

"And you're sure you want to marry one of them?"

"Yes, Dad. Conner and I are meant to be together."

"Meant to be together? You're sounding like a movie, Tina. Not like a woman who has thought this all through."

"Trust me, Dad. I've looked at this from every angle. And I will admit, initially I said yes mainly because I wanted to get away from Robyn. But it didn't take long at all to see that there was a lot more to my feelings for Conner. Male shifters start dreaming of their mate when she turns twenty one. But he'd first met me weeks before my birthday. Without knowing I was his mate, he attempted to help me. So, it's not just that we were predestined to be together. He truly cares for me, protects me above all else. You know he got injured getting me out of the fire? A burning roof beam fell into him, knocked him into a wall. He'd wrapped his turnout coat around me so his shoulder copped the full force and heat of it. But even then, he didn't stop. He knew I couldn't get myself out. He pushed the beam off, grabbed me up, and lunged out the door. Dad, if he wasn't supernatural, we'd both be dead."

"What about you? Are you one of them now too?"

"No, Dad. Conner told me it's a DNA thing. I'll always be fully human."

She searched her father's gaze and saw he was worried and confused.

"It's okay, Dad. Conner makes me really happy. Even Dr Reid said I'm looking better."

"I just worry about you, sweet pea. I didn't see Robyn for who she was, I didn't protect you from her. I won't allow a man to get a hold of you and hurt you more."

"Oh, Dad. Stop blaming yourself for Robyn's behavior. And I know in my soul that Conner would never hurt me."

A knock on the doorframe brought a halt to their conversation. Tina hoped her dad could forgive himself for Robyn. She didn't blame him, no one did. Robyn was crazy all on her own. Unfortunately, Robyn had become obsessed with her dad and her craziness snowballed from there.

"Sorry to interrupt, Mr Anderson, but I need to talk to you."

Tina watched the police officer enter the room and approach the bed.

"I'm Detective Alex Ross, I'm handling Ms Robyn Taylor's case and need your side of things."

Tina smiled up at the officer. "I'll leave you two to discuss it. I need to go check on Conner."

"Thank you, Ms Anderson. I believe Conner is down the hall making sure Robyn doesn't escape."

Tina felt the blood drain from her face. "She's not under arrest yet?"

He chuckled with a slight shake of his head, "Oh, she's under arrest all right. We're still compiling a full list of charges against her, but she'll be getting locked up soon enough. Her medical issues need seeing to first. She is cuffed to the bed and has two officers at her bedside. She's not going anywhere. Conner is simply being over-protective. All his kind are that way, especially when it comes to their women."

He gave them both a wink and Tina was relieved he knew about the shifters. She wasn't sure her dad was up to making up something viable to cover the facts.

"Well, I'll go do my best to drag him away from hassling your men then."

He gave her a nod and smile. "I'm sure they'd appreciate that. They get nervous with a cat pacing around them."

"Perfectly understandable."

She rolled out into the hall and began looking for her man. Thankfully, the hospital was small and it only took a matter of minutes to find him pacing the hallway outside a shut door. He looked so tense, clenching and unclenching his fists. Adele was standing in front of the closed door, talking softly to Conner and he was shaking his head.

"Conner?"

At the sound of her voice, his head snapped up as his feet ground to a halt.

"Baby doll."

She watched his powerful strides as he strode to her. Damn, he was so sexy when he was on a mission. In one smooth movement, he scooped her up out of her chair and brought her up to his chest. A low purr emanated from him as he nuzzled into her neck.

"Let's go back to your place, Conner. You're creating a scene here."

She smiled as she noticed the light blush staining his cheeks when he pulled back from her. He gently returned her to the chair.

"You know the police have Robyn covered. She's not going anywhere."

Adele threw in her support that they leave the hospital for some fresh air and Conner looked a little defeated. Tina almost felt sorry for him, being ganged up on by women.

"Okay, okay. We're going. You'll let me know as soon as anything happens?"

"Of course I will, Conner. Go, take your mate out and relax a little."

Tina waved her thanks to Adele as Conner wheeled her toward the exit and out into the midday sun.

Chapter Ten

Conner could feel the ache in his shoulder as he pulled Tina's chair from the back of his Prado. He wished it would hurry up and heal already. With everything that was going on he couldn't afford to be anything but at the top of his game. After he settled Tina into her chair, he locked the car up and walked her down the main street, staying by her side but allowing her to control their speed. She needed clothes, and they needed somewhere of their own. He knew Tina was uncomfortable sleeping with him under his parents' roof. He saw the bright green and yellow of the real estate agent office just ahead.

"Do you mind if we stop in at the real estate place for a minute?"

"Ah, yeah, sure."

She looked so fragile in that moment, he was certain she was thinking about the burned shell they'd visited that morning. He'd crept in and grabbed a couple of small things that they'd seen but it wasn't much. He hadn't wanted to touch too much, especially in the front of the house where the fire had started. Nor did he want the remaining structure to fall in on him.

He cupped her face in his palm. "We're going to need

a place of our own, unless you like living with my parents?"

"Ah, no. Don't want to live with anybody's parents forever. Just, it's all so quick and so much has happened. I need a little time."

"Take all the time you need, baby doll. How about I leave you at the clothes store while I nip in and get some brochures? We can look them over at home, whenever we want to. No pushy agents to deal with that way."

She smiled shyly up at him. "That sounds better. I don't want some agent pressuring either of us into some rundown shack while we're not thinking clearly."

"Wise words, indeed."

They continued in comfortable silence until they reached a large clothing store. Kissing her on the cheek, he went on to the agent as she went inside. Not wanting to be parted from her, he hurried into the office, quickly acquired brochures for relevant houses and made his way back to his mate. He found her looking sad as she rolled down an isle toward him.

"Hey, baby doll, what's wrong?"

"I, um, can't afford anything. I didn't think before we came in. I have no money. I'll have to talk to Dad-"

Conner cut her off by pressing his lips against her soft mouth. He pulled back slightly to whisper, "Hush, sweetheart. I've got it covered. And before you tell me I'm not allowed, I'm going to be your husband, your mate. It's my duty to provide for you. Let me do this for you? Please."

She leaned in, delivering a quick kiss before she responded. "When you put it like that, I can't very well refuse now can I?"

"So glad you understand."

His heart lightened as she giggled and headed back down the aisle. He'd always hated going shopping with women, but with Tina, he soon found himself enjoying the experience. Tina didn't fluff around but went straight to what she wanted and found her size. He answered questions when asked and didn't think he'd made any blunders with his answers. Well, she was still talking to him when they reached the checkout, so it was looking good.

Tina held her bags on her lap and Conner pushed her out to his car. The afternoon sun was shining bright and a fresh breeze blew past them. He drew in a deep breath and let his happiness radiate throughout him. He had his mate, and she was safe with him.

"The sun feels so nice against your skin, doesn't it?"

"Sure does. The sun hasn't got that summer bite yet. There's nothing quite like spring sunshine."

It didn't take him long to get everything loaded up and they headed back to his parents' place. As he drove, he slipped one hand onto Tina's thigh; she placed hers over the top, interlacing their fingers. He loved touching her, feeling her close to him. He moved his hand to change gears, and she kept hers with his the whole time. He grinned like a fool, knowing she didn't want to break the contact either.

It didn't take long for them to arrive. He was almost disappointed that the trip was so short. As soon as he saw both his parents' cars missing from the garage, his mood picked up.

"What you are grinning about? You look like a cat that's just got the cream."

He turned his gaze on Tina and watched as she shuddered under the intensity.

"Not yet. But I am a cat who is intent on getting his cream. We've got the house to ourselves for the rest of the afternoon, baby doll."

She returned his grin. "Is that right? So, why are we sitting out here in the car then?"

With a low growl, he jumped from the car and prowled around to her door. Ignoring the chair and the shopping, he scooped her up and strode toward the house. He was a man on a mission.

Tina snuggled into Conner as he lifted her from her chair into the car. She was worn out from her session in the pool with Nina, but she also felt content. Finally, she was making headway with her rehab. The talented physio was sure Tina would be walking soon—albeit with crutches for a while.

Conner kissed the top of her head as she rubbed her face against his hard pectoral. "You all right, baby doll?"

"Yeah, just worn out from the session."

He placed her on the seat before he pulled back to cup her face. "I'm so proud of you, Tina. You've come so far in such a short amount of time. Let's head home. I've got another lot of brochures to look through, if you're up to it."

She smiled up at her fiancé. He'd been scouring the town for the perfect house. He had saved quite the nest egg and wanted to buy a home for them. But he was so damn picky! Tina would have been happy with any of the ones he'd brought to her to check over. It was fun to watch him pull apart each property, listing everything good and bad about each one. She'd been living with Conner and his parents for a full week now. Jake and Sophie were lovely. They gave her and Conner plenty of alone time and privacy, and were kind and considerate to her all the time.

Her dad had stayed there too for a couple of days, but he was now in a rental house near their old place. He was currently in negotiations with the builders that the insurance company had sent out to quote on fixing the house. Funny how things turned out sometimes. He'd been chatting to the foreman about needing work. Ken, the foreman, had been saying how hard it was to find workers with a good worth ethic. Her dad had a lot of experience with fixing mechanical things on the rigs he'd always worked. Ken was sure he'd pick up building houses in no time, so her dad now had a job on the island. No more leaving for offshore rigs.

A shudder ran through her as she remembered some of the not-so-good things that had happened in the last week. Robyn had been granted bail. She'd shut the salon and had disappeared along with Barbara. Tina prayed they had both left town and were far away from Rosebery, but she knew in her heart they hadn't.

"You cold?"

Conner flicked up the heat in the car. "Not really. I just had a bad thought run through my mind, that's all."

"What bad thought was that, baby doll?"

"Just about what Robyn is up to."

"The police are looking for her. She has to slip up soon. She's too unstable to remain hidden. And until she does get caught, you will always have someone with you to keep you safe. I promise, she won't get to you again."

Thankfully, that was when they pulled up outside his house. Tina needed a change of subject. "So, how many houses did you find today?"

"Just the one today. But it's a real gem."

She chuckled at the proud look on Conner's face as he helped her into the chair and pushed her inside. He had turned finding their house into mission impossible; his 'had to have' list was getting rather long.

They moved into the lounge room and Conner handed her a folded slip of paper. She unfolded it to find a large picture of a house surrounded by the most spectacular view of the Cradle Mountains.

"Oh my goodness! Look at that view."

"Yeah, it's the view that caught my attention first off. It's got no steps, wide sliding doors in the back. Open plan living areas. Three bedrooms."

Chuckling, she cut him off, "I can read Conner. It

looks lovely."

The house had a cottage feel to it. Something about its freshly painted cream colored weather-boards and the green iron roof, which also looked new.

"It's even got a shed for you to play in." She teased.

"Yeah, that also caught my attention. A man has to have a shed."

"So, we're going to go have a look at it then?"

"Yeah, I've arranged with the agent to go around there tomorrow morning. You don't have a rehab session tomorrow do you?"

"No, I have tomorrow off. Nina told me I can't push too hard or I could end up injuring myself. Tomorrow is my relaxation day."

Conner's face showed his concern, "You're not in pain now are you? Do you need to go lay down for a bit? Mum should be back any minute from her tutoring lesson with Kelly and no doubt she'll set about making a fuss out of dinner."

"Yeah, a lie down sounds good. Will you join me—don't go getting ideas, not with your mum due home. I just want your arms around me for a while."

His face softened as he approached. "Of course, baby doll. I love having you in my arms. Any excuse to repeat the event, I'm there with bells on."

She laughed as her mind spat out an interesting mental image. "Well, you are a cat. I'm sure a collar with a bell could be arranged."

"Man, are you in a mood. Cheeky woman."

Leaving the chair behind, he carried her to their bedroom and laid her down on the soft mattress. Moments later he spooned up beside her, pulling her back into the cradle of his body. He kissed the nape of her neck and she sighed at the warmth it infused throughout her body.

"I love you, Conner."

He pressed his lips to her skin again and whispered against her, "And I you. Now, close those pretty emerald eyes and get some rest. I'm not going anywhere."

Robyn paced the room, her mind a tumble of thoughts, all tripping over each other. She couldn't keep them straight. She shook out her hands, hoping to shake away some of the clutter in her mind with it. It eased only slightly but was enough for her to focus.

Barbara should have returned by now. How hard could it be to find out where Dale was staying now that he'd moved out of the White's place? She had to get to Dale without those damn do-gooders around. She had to explain, make him see they were meant to be together. Then he could tell the police to drop the charges. Gah! The police had listed off several charges, then told her there may be more once the investigation was finished. She didn't bother remembering any of them. She would be free once Dale told them it was okay.

A car pulling up outside the front of the small cabin brought her to the door. The caravan park was small, with only a couple of permanent cabins. Nice and private, hopefully secluded enough the cops wouldn't find her. Perhaps skipping bail wasn't her best option, but it was done now. No way was she checking in with the police station every day, or staying away from Dale. She opened the door just as Barbara approached. "What did you find out?"

Barbara didn't answer as she came in and dropped her bag on the table. The wait was grating on Robyn's already frayed nerves.

"Well?"

"Calm down, I'll tell you in a minute. Damn it, you can't even let me walk in the door before you start at me? I don't have to help you, you know?"

Robyn just glared at her friend. Now that the salon was shut Barbara had no job. Because she'd always lived week to week, spending all her pay, she had no savings. Robyn had simply promised her a payout once this was all over. It also helped that as Barbara was the one who posted bail, the police would be after her too, now that Robyn had skipped out.

Barbara huffed and rolled her eyes. "Fine. Be that way. Dale is renting a place on Pitt Street. Number twenty-nine. He's landed himself a job with the building company that's fixing up his place, so he's not going anywhere in a hurry. Looks like he was serious about giving up the offshore work. Oh, and that shrink? What's her name?"

"Jennifer Reid." She could hear the snarl in her voice but didn't care. The woman was trying to steal her man out from under her. And that would not do.

"Yeah, that's the one. They've been spending a lot of time together. Can't possibly be only appointments about Tina's welfare. Word is, they're dating."

Robyn's vision clouded with the sudden intense desire to go out and hurt Jennifer. How dare she take what was hers!

"What are you planning on doing now?"

"I need to approach Dale when he's alone. But getting him alone is going to be tricky..."

"Well, I also managed to find out that he's taking the afternoon off work tomorrow. He's taking Tina out for a picnic apparently. I bet Conner and Jennifer will tag along, but you might still get him on his own at some point."

"Or you could do something to hold up the others, allow me a few moments with my man."

"I'm sure that can be arranged."

The sly grin on Barbara's face was surely a reflection of her own. Finally she would get what was rightfully hers.

Conner stood back to allow Tina to lead the way. The agent was already inside waiting for them. She stopped on the back veranda and looked away from the house.

"Look at that view, Conner. Can you imagine waking up to see that every morning?"

He came up beside her and ran his hand through her hair before resting his hand possessively around her neck. "Yeah, I can and so long as you're looking at it beside me, it'll be paradise."

He thoroughly enjoyed the pink tinge on her cheeks as Tina wheeled the rest of the way inside the house. He followed behind her and met up with the agent, Marlee, inside.

He dutifully followed behind the women as Marlee gave them the spiel for each room. Conner already knew everything he could about the house. He'd thoroughly researched its history and all of its features, but Tina needed to hear it all. He needed to watch for her reaction to the house. He had a feeling she'd agree to anything just to keep him happy. He had been very fussy about choosing them a home.

At the end of the tour Marlee left them alone to chat.

"So, what do you think?"

"The whole house is beautiful, and I can get everywhere in the chair. Not that I'll be in it for long, but still."

He swiftly bent down to kiss her lips. "And the view is amazing."

"Hmmm, yeah that too. I like the kitchen, it's all open plan with plenty of room to entertain, but it's not so big I'm going to be spending all my time cleaning the damn thing."

He chuckled at her reasoning. She could be so endearing with her logic some times.

"So you'd be happy if I bought it for us then?"

"What do *you* think about it? You barely paid any

attention to what Marlee was saying."

"That's because I didn't need to. I already knew everything she told you. This place had my tick of approval before we arrived today. I was simply waiting for yours before I put an offer in."

"I can only guess how much you know about this place by now. You'd probably be able to tell me how many nails were used when it was built."

"Not quite, baby doll, but pretty close. Shall we go round up the agent and buy ourselves a house then?"

"Sounds good to me!"

The huge grin and sparkle in her eyes made him feel like he was ten feet tall. He loved nothing more than seeing his mate so utterly happy, especially when he was responsible for it.

It didn't take long for Marlee to put their offer to the owners. She was even kind enough to explain about the house fire and request an earlier settlement than they had stated. Having already moved out, the owners were more than happy to have a quick settlement. Conner was incredibly grateful his father had encouraged his sons to save as much as they could from an early age. He had the hundred and fifty thousand dollars required to buy the property in his bank account so they wouldn't need to worry about a loan.

In a matter of hours they had the details all sorted. Settlement would be in thirty days, and the owners didn't mind them moving in beforehand. Marlee suggested a rental agreement for the four week period, just to cover all the bases, legally speaking. Unbelievably, he walked out of the real estate office with the keys to the house.

Amazing.

"Well, we certainly have something to tell your father at the picnic now. Then we get to go furniture shopping."

Tina laughed nervously. "I can't believe you just bought a house."

"*We* just bought a house, sweetheart."

"C'mon lets go meet up with your dad and celebrate."

Conner vibrated with joy as he helped Tina into the car, knowing he would definitely have to go for a run later. He'd ring Dom after their dinner and see if he wanted to go out tonight, after Tina was safely home with his folks. With all the stress and excitement going on in these last few weeks, his leopard was desperate to be set free.

Conner enjoyed breathing in his mate's scent during the short drive to the picnic spot where they were meeting Dale. It was at the top of a cliff that dropped off into the lake. The cliff wasn't too high up from the water, but had a great view and would suit them perfectly. It had a car park nearby and a small, grassy area between the scrub and the cliff edge where they could relax and enjoy their early dinner before watching the sunset.

His contented and happy mood quickly vanished and was replaced with a feeling of dread as they approached the car park. There were large yellow scrape marks and dents along the passenger side of Dale's black Hilux. It looked like the vehicle had been rammed from an angle.

Conner guessed they'd been driving through a Y junction, when someone came down the adjoining road and ran into them.

"What the hell caused that?" He could hear the rising panic in Tina's voice.

"I don't know, baby doll. But I'm guessing Robyn found your dad."

He jumped free of the car, left the chair behind and gathered Tina in his arms before he locked up and headed to the picnic spot.

"Why didn't you just put me in the chair and wheel me?"

"Well, you know how I like you in my arms, so any excuse. And the chair would just get stuck in this path. It's easier for me to carry you."

He gave her temple a light kiss as he continued his way through the scrub. He heard Dale's angry voice before he saw him. Dale was definitely not in a good mood, which Conner fully understood, considering the state of his car.

"Hell yeah I'm filing a report. The crazy bitch ran straight into us! I'm just thankful the junction was at such an angle. If she'd hit us straight on at that speed, Jennifer would have been seriously injured or killed."

Tina cringed in his arms at her father's harsh voice. They entered the clearing to find Dale standing protectively beside Jennifer with one hand on his hip and the other holding a phone to his ear. Jennifer was sitting with her knees up and her arms wrapped around them.

She looked uninjured, but definitely shaken up. Her head was up watching them as Conner stepped into the open. She was on full alert to any danger. Conner could sense her leopard close to the surface, ready to pounce in order to protect.

"It's just us. What the hell happened?"

"Barbara happened. She's as crazy as Robyn. She was stationary at the lights, then I guess when she saw me in Dale's car it flicked her switch and she floored it straight into us. I looked out as I heard the wheels squeal. Her car stopped after the impact, but we weren't hanging around to take names and numbers. You should have seen her face. Even professionally I've never seen anyone with that level of rage."

With a growl, Dale hung up the phone. "The cops went around to the accident scene and picked up Barbara, still trying to get her car started after hitting us. So that's one down. Robyn's still on the loose though. Damn it. How can one woman cause so much damn trouble? It's getting bloody ridiculous."

"You're Robyn's obsession, Dale. She believes you are hers and she'll stop at nothing to get you. She is a very ill woman. No doubt she'll be diagnosed as having a psychotic break when she gets caught. Thankfully, it would be a conflict of interest for me to treat her."

Jennifer shuddered and Dale was quick to drop to her side and wrap her in his arms. Conner didn't fail to notice how she leaned into the embrace. As a Widow Mate, Jennifer was free to date whoever she wanted. Conner was happy to see her hook up with Dale. They'd both been dealt a rough hand when it came to love and would make a good couple.

Conner gently placed Tina on the picnic rug before settling down beside her.

"Are you two sure you're okay? I mean, we can postpone this to another day."

"No, don't be silly. We're fine, just a little shaken up. Please, tell us about the house you were going to look at this morning."

He watched as Dale stood again and resumed his pacing. Tina gave her dad a worried glance before she started telling them all about the house.

"Sounds like you really fancy the place. Have you put an offer in on it?"

Dale seemed to relax as he joined the conversation, but continued to stand while they all sat.

"Well, we did more than that. The owners have already accepted our offer, and as the house is empty we're moving in as soon as we can get some furniture together. We'll be renting it for a month until the settlement goes through."

"Wow! Well, congratulations. I'm glad things are finally going well for you, sweet pea. And Conner, I can't thank you enough for looking after my girl like you have."

Looking to the ground, Conner felt heat rise in his cheeks; he really didn't like dealing with emotions. Tina brushed her knuckles over his heated skin, lessening his embarrassment. "It's my pleasure, Dale. She's my whole world."

Conner was still squirming under the attention of his mate's father when he caught the scent of Robyn. He leapt to his feet as a shrill high-pitched scream ripped through the air. Before he could make a move, Robyn came out of the tree line and collided into Dale. Unprepared for the impact, Dale reeled backward and they both went over the cliff, splashing into the lake below. Tina screamed and started to pull herself toward the edge. He snatched her up before he glanced around for Jennifer. He just caught a glimpse of her as she pounced off the cliff in leopard form to the lake below.

He brought Tina to the edge, as close as he dared, and searched the water below for any sign of Dale, Jennifer or Robyn. Thankfully the cliff was only a few meters high. It hadn't been a huge fall for them. The lake was deep in this part so he wouldn't have hit the bottom and hurt himself, however the risk of drowning was very real. Conner watched as Jennifer swam to shore. Dale had a tight grip around Jennifer's strong neck, his hands buried deep in her fur.

"There they are! I see them. I was so worried when he plunged over the edge."

"Yeah, baby. He'll be fine. Leopards are strong swimmers. No way would Jennifer let him drown. Let's get down to them."

She nodded and clung tighter to his neck, never taking her gaze from her father as he moved down the path toward the shore below.

Chapter Eleven

Robyn hadn't thought, she'd simply acted. Seeing that bitch Jennifer so close to her man clouded her vision red in rage. Then Conner flew up to his feet and looked straight at her hiding spot with death in his gaze. She knew her time was up so she'd run to Dale. It wasn't so much a plan as it was running on instinct.

Turns out her instincts sucked.

As enjoyable as it was having her body pressed against Dale's for those few seconds before they flew over the cliff edge, Robyn wasn't sure it was worth it. Dale had now shoved her away from him and she was freefalling on her own.

With a loud splash, she hit the icy cold water of the lake and sank below the surface. Kicking frantically, she struggled to make her way to the top. Holding her breath, she pulled her thick jacket free from her body then swam to the surface. She broke free from the water with a gasp and without looking around her, made her way to the closest shore. Her brain on survival mode, she didn't even think of Dale until she was pulling her tired body from the icy water and onto the small stones that made up the lake's edge.

Fear froze her lungs as she flicked her head around and searched for any sign of him.

"Dad!"

Tina's panicked filled voice reached her and Robyn turned to watch the shore on the other side of the cliff. The breath she was holding whooshed from her as she tried to process what she was seeing.

"What the hell?" She mumbled to herself.

A large black and white cat—easily the size of a leopard—was standing over Dale, who lay on the shore. The cat's large head lowered toward him and Robyn's hand reached out for him as a sob caught in her throat. The animal was going to kill him and she was too far away to do anything about it. As Conner came up to the pair with Tina in his arms, the beast stepped back and sat close by.

"What the hell is going on over there?"

Dale sat up coughing, and Conner lowered Tina to the ground by Dale's side. Jealousy ripped through her as Dale gathered Tina into his embrace.

It should be me he holds that closely.

Conner shrugging out of his shirt caught her attention. Frowning in confusion, she watched as he walked up to the cat. He was no doubt saying something to it, but she couldn't hear from this distance.

"Oh hell no! That can't possibly be real!"

A blue haze formed around the animal before it turned to a person. Not just any person but Jennifer. A naked Jennifer. All thoughts of how people could change to animals flew from her mind as Robyn growled low in her throat. How dare she parade around her man naked! Jennifer quickly grabbed the shirt Conner held behind his back. *Such a gentleman,* she thought sarcastically as he turned away from her to allow her to dress. Thankfully Conner was a big man and the shirt hung down nearly to Jennifer's knees.

Taking a couple of deep breaths, Robyn managed to calm down a little. She watched as Conner picked up Tina from Dale's lap and Jennifer helped Dale stand. Fury raced through her blood yet again as she could clearly see Dale lean into Jennifer, allowing the woman to help him up the slope toward the car park.

Once they were out of her sight, she focused on herself. She was saturated obviously, but hadn't realized how cold she was. Her arms held a blue tinge and she shivered as icy fingers pricked over her body. She forced herself to her feet and made her way through the bush. She didn't have her car so would have to trek back to the cabin. It hadn't taken her long to walk here that morning, but she doubted, wet and cold like she was, that it would be such an easy return trip.

As she made her way past the car park, she paused and watched as Dale dried off with a picnic blanket. He'd stripped off his jacket and shirt and stood barefoot. Robyn sighed in feminine appreciation as she observed the ripple of his muscles as he moved. She was close enough to hear their conversation as Conner handed Dale some clothes.

"Here you go. They'll be a little big but should do the job. You never know when you're going to need to shift so we generally keep a couple sets of clothes in our cars."

What the hell? Conner was one of the weird cat people too?

Her lip curled up as Conner handed Jennifer a pair of pants and she slipped them on.

"Guess I should start keeping a bag in Dale's car. Thanks, Conner."

Dale pulled Jennifer into his arms and kissed her temple. Robyn dug her fingers into a tree trunk to prevent herself from bolting out to him again. Her rage continued to simmer as he stroked Jennifer's face and declared his thanks for her saving him. This was not how it was meant to be! A tear ran down her face as she watched the intimate moment. Loud sirens broke through the area and Conner declared it was the police responding to his call and that they would be searching for her.

That's my cue to leave.

Wiping tears from her face, she quietly made her way from Dale and toward the cabin. With each step she grew more angry and confused. Dale was hers. She was sure they were destined to be together. Somehow that cat woman had put a spell on him. Robyn just needed to get him alone. Surely if Jennifer wasn't close by, she wouldn't have a hold over him?

As she slowly plodded through the dense scrub, she thought over what she'd seen. The woman was a cat. Snow leopards were black and white like that, weren't they? Like everyone in town, Robyn had heard the rumors of big cats running through the Cradle Mountain National Park. Also like everyone else, she'd assumed them nothing more than stories made up to bring in tourists and to frighten children into staying close to their parents.

Apparently, they weren't rumors at all and she was going to have to be very careful from now on.

Adding a flattened box to the pile in the lounge, Tina sighed.

"That's the last box."

It hadn't taken long to move. All of her stuff had been lost in the fire. Having lived at home with his folks, Conner didn't have much either. The furniture shop had delivered all their purchases yesterday, so today it hadn't taken long at all to unpack their few belongings and all the many housewarming presents all their helpers had brought with them.

She felt the warmth of Conner's hands as he laid them on her shoulders before he kissed the top of her head.

"We've officially moved in then."

"Yep, and all the helpers have disappeared leaving us officially alone."

"Hmmm, indeed we are."

Turning her head, she watched as he moved to the couch and sat down.

"Come over and join me?"

He had a serious look in his gaze that had Tina more

than a little curious—and nervous. Once she came to a stop in front of him, he took her hands in his.

"There's something I need to ask you."

His gaze focused on their joined hands and she felt him twist her engagement ring back and forth with his thumb.

"What is it, Conner? You know you can be totally honest with me about anything."

Silence hung in the air as Conner frowned down at her ring. She was starting to get quite concerned when he finally lifted his head and held her gaze. After the whole shape shifter thing, Tina didn't think there could possibly be any more huge declarations he'd have to make to her.

"Will you mate with me?"

Tina tilted her head in confusion. "I don't understand what you mean, Conner. I already said yes to getting married."

"Mating is different. It's more permanent."

"In my book, marriage is permanent."

His gaze softened and he raised a hand to cup her face. "I know, baby doll. Trust me, it is in my book too. But mating is a shifter thing. It's us bonding together. Damn, I'm making a mess of explaining this." He paused to rub his hands on his legs before taking hers back into his grip. "Have you noticed when we climax together, claws sprout from my right hand?"

She felt the blood drain from her face. *Claws?*

"Can't say I have. I'm generally a little busy at the time. What would you need claws for, Conner?"

"The Marking. It's part of Mating. I'll mark you and you me. It's a physical sign of our love and bond for each other."

Tina was grateful she was in her chair, because had she been standing, she'd be passed out.

"You want to *scratch* me? With your, no doubt huge, leopard claws?"

"I wouldn't really be scratching you. It's based in magic and doesn't hurt at all. You'll be left with four scratch marks revealing leopard spots. It'll look a lot like my shoulder does."

"And how do I mark you? I don't change into a cat."

"And you won't start changing into one now either. The magic of the mating flows through me to you. You'll have claws just this once."

Tina pulled away from Conner to roll around the room. She needed some movement to get her mind turning over. He wanted to *mate* with her. Okay, he was a shifter so part animal. She could understand how that entailed some extra things along the way.

But scratching? Marking each other?

That was over the top...wasn't it?

The room's light reflected from her ring, catching her eye. She stopped and looked down at her hand. She would wear that ring for the rest of her days, to show the world she was married and to ward off any other man who might think to try to seduce her. Her breath caught as the realization hit, the marking would be no different. Marriage was forever as far as she was concerned, and she loved Conner. If getting a pain free tattoo in the process of laying claim to him was what had to happen, then great. She did like Conner's scar—she hated that it happened, that the fire had burned his skin—but the leopard spots looked sexy as hell.

She spun her chair around so she faced Conner. He had a pained expression and held his hands in tight fists against his knees. His whole body looked tense, like he was preparing for a fight. Her heart clenched, he was preparing for her rejection of the mating; of him.

She went to him and his knees parted to allow her closer access to him. She scooted forward in her chair before she leaned in to cup his face in both her palms. "I love you, Conner. Yes, I will mate with you."

She pressed her lips against his and felt the shudder that ran through him. She squealed in surprise when he pulled her from her chair and into his lap. He swallowed the sound as he took control of the kiss. Pushing the chair away with his foot, he stood with her securely in his arms and rushed to the bedroom. Tina couldn't help the giggle that escaped. Her heart was full to bursting with happiness and love.

With a firm grip on her hips, he stood her at the side of their bed and continued his passionate kiss. She trailed her hands over his back before seeking out the bottom of his shirt and sliding beneath. He broke the kiss. "Can you stand on your own?"

His voice had taken a husky tone with his arousal and she felt a warmth bloom in her core in response.

"Yeah, I'm fine to stand for quite a while now."

"It'll only be a minute or two."

He stepped back from her and tore at his shirt. The second his chest was bared to her, her hand reached for him. As if it had a mind of its own, it sought him out. He closed his eyes as a slight tremor ran through his body. Snapping his eyes open, he quickly moved to remove her shirt. It was lifted up and over her head in seconds. Her pants received similar treatment. He took a moment to run his heated gaze over her body, now covered only in lacy underwear.

"You are so sexy, baby doll."

Tina was about to combust. She was sure she'd melt into a puddle on the floor if Conner didn't hurry up. She unclasped her bra as he reached for the button of his jeans. She shrugged out of the lace, allowing it to float to the floor. He opened his fly and pushed the denim from his hips. His jeans dropped to the floor with a soft thud.

"You are gorgeous, Conner. Every inch of you is perfect."

"I was about to say the same about you, sweetheart. So beautiful and all mine."

He hooked his thumbs in the sides of his boxer briefs and Tina feared she'd swallow her tongue as his erection sprung free. Moments later Conner had his arms firmly wrapped around her as he took possession of her mouth. The heated passion running through her body began to overwhelm her, her knees buckled and Conner held her weight against him.

Conner absorbed the feeling of having Tina willingly rely on his strength to hold her up. He was caveman enough to bask in the sensation. He had his mate so turned on she couldn't stand. Purring, he moved from her mouth to press kisses over her cheek and down her neck. She arched beneath him, giving him better access. He playfully nipped at her throat before he laid her down on their bed. He stripped her knickers from her toned legs, laying kisses over the scars down her thigh. Once he had her naked, he prowled over her body. She stretched beneath him in a decidedly feline manner, her hands above her head as she arched her back. Her breasts were thrust up before him and he simply couldn't resist. He pulled one into his mouth, flicking his tongue over the tight peak until she writhed beneath him with her hands in his hair. He kissed his way over to the other, lavishing that one with equal attention. He heard her begin to pant and felt her move her thighs against each other, obviously seeking some relief.

He shifted down her body, desperate for a taste of his mate. Her scent continued to fill his senses as he lowered himself and took a lick. Her eyes flew open, and with a raised eyebrow she glanced down at him.

"Didn't I tell you? I can shift just my tongue. There's nothing quite like a feline's rough tongue to fully taste one's mate." He paused for another lick and took delight in her reaction. Her head pressed back into the pillows as her hands gripped the sheet on either side while her body convulsed with ripples of obvious pleasure.

"Uh huh."

He chuckled at her moaned response before he focused back on her sweet heat. Purring loudly, he licked and suckled at her core, taking as much of her as he could down his throat. He would never get enough of drinking in his mate. Her muscles began to tighten as he felt her fingers slide into his hair. She gripped him to her as she shattered under his touch. As she quivered in the aftermath of her climax, he sat back on his knees and watched her. She had a contented, sated smile on her lips and a rosy glow to her face and neck.

"Roll over, baby doll. I need to be inside you."

Without hesitation, his sweet mate languidly rolled over then pushed back so she was on her hands and knees.

"Is your leg okay to hold that position? You can lie flat on a pillow if it's more comfortable."

"Please, Conner, just take me. I need you. My rehab has been going well, I'll be fine. If it starts to hurt, I promise I'll tell you."

He leaned in to lay a gentle kiss on her lower spine, just above her perfectly toned bottom.

"Do you want me to use a condom? Because I really want to be able to feel all of you when we mate."

He felt the shudder go through her and heard her breathing accelerate. "You, I need you. No condom."

Conner closed his eyes against the overwhelming emotions that swirled inside him.

"I love you, Tina. I'm going to love you forever."

He shuffled forward closer to her and lined his heavy erection up with her slick entrance. Pressing in, he shook with the pleasure of feeling her feminine heat envelope him for the first time without a latex barrier. He wrapped an arm beneath her stomach to help support her weight as he began to slowly pump into her. Unable to resist, he slid his free hand up to tweak her nipple. She clenched down on him as she gasped.

It felt like paradise.

He gave her other nipple the same treatment and enjoyed her reaction again. Within moments he could feel himself climbing ever closer to his climax. Leaving her breasts, he straightened his spine, gripped her hips and began to thrust faster into her. With his left hand he reached around to press against her sensitive bundle of nerves. Three flicks later she shattered around him, pulling him with her straight over the ledge into bliss. His hand was firmly over her right hip as magic tingled and his claws sprouted. He dragged his fingers back, leaving an arc of scratch marks over her hipbone.

Pulling from her core, he gently rolled her over on her back. He picked up her right hand and let her see the claws that were now where her nails had been. As she gasped in awe, he placed her hand over his heart.

"Scratch me, Tina. Mark me as yours, right over my heart."

She curled her fingers and dragged them down his chest. The magic sparked through his entire being. His breath caught, and as he watched Tina writhe under the same sensations, he felt himself harden for her all over again. He covered her body with his, thrusting inside her in one strong move. He could barely hear her moan through his roar of possession.

She was his.

Claimed fully as his mate.

No other would *ever* touch her.

Magic flowed throughout her body, her fingers tickled as the claws disappeared and her nails reappeared. Conner's hard body was pressed against her. He'd buried himself within her in one strong stroke, and now she moaned, as his animalistic roar filled the room. He pounded into her, dominating her. Her body was overwhelmed with sensation. Her mind spun with all that was happening.

Conner lifted up on his arms to look down at her. Her gaze wandered from his face to his chest, and she raised her hand to trace the mark over his heart. Four wide scratch marks revealed his leopard spots over his heart. She pressed her palm against it and a small jolt of magic ran though her again. He closed his eyes and his whole body tightened above her. Obviously he'd felt the jolt too.

Continuing his thrusts into her, he lowered his head to torment her nipples and breasts. Tossing her head back and forth on the pillow, she moaned as the coil in her belly began to tighten impossibly tight. He kneeled as his strokes sped up. The new angle took him deeper inside her. She watched, lost in a daze of passion as his hand moved to her clit. He flicked and teased it until she was bucking against him. She screamed as she flew apart for the third time that night. His roar once again filled the air as she felt his warmth fill her womb. She hoped she was fertile at the moment. The only way this experience could be sweeter would be if they had created life.

"That was amazing. Even though I'd been told what would happen, that was so much more. I love you."

Conner rested his head against her chest and she managed to raise her hand to run her fingers through his sweat-drenched hair. "I love you too, Conner. And yeah, that was spectacular."

He raised his head to stare up at her. She could see love and desire, along with male smugness and pride. Her man was macho enough to be delighted at having marked her. She was girly enough to relish the fact he wanted to mark her as his forever. He gently, reverently, kissed her as his palm covered her mark, the magic tingling once again.

"Let's go have a shower, shall we?"

"Only if you carry me."

"Of course, baby doll. I'd carry you everywhere if you'd let me."

Tina relaxed into Conner's embrace as he scooped her from the bed and headed toward the bathroom. He set her on the bench seat he'd installed for her and grabbed the handheld shower. After adjusting the water, he rinsed her off and handed her the showerhead. He lathered up his hands and proceeded to clean every inch of her. His touch on her sensitive skin revved her up. By the time he was washing her feet, she was panting with her arousal. Now on his knees, he spread her thighs and buried his face between them, suckling on her aroused flesh. She cried out as he nipped at her clit, the sensation enough to push her over yet again. She shuddered beneath him as he lapped at her, drinking down her liquid heat once more.

He rose from the floor and she forced her eyes to open so she could watch the play of his muscles as he took the showerhead from her and washed himself. Leaning heavily against the wall she didn't realize she'd dozed off until she jerked awake as Conner picked her up from the seat.

"Let's go back to bed, sweetheart."

He snagged a towel on his way back to the bedroom and set her on the end of the mattress before he carefully dried her off. He finger combed her hair before he tucked her in beneath the covers. She cracked her lids open just enough to see him dry his spectacular body before he moved to crawl into the bed beside her. He rolled her on to her side before tucking her in against him. He slid his hand down to cup her mating mark and the tingle jolted her system as she drifted off into a very sated, content sleep.

Tina slowly surfaced to the sound of Conner's angry voice on the phone.

"What do you mean she's not been found? You told us she'd be caught in no time, or her body found. That was three days ago!"

Oh hell no, Robyn was still on the loose? Heaven only knew what stunt she'd pull next. Would her dad ever be safe from her? A sob caught in her throat and she rolled to bury her face into the pillow, then curled into as tight a ball as she could while emotions battled inside her. She was feeling so overwhelmed, the last weeks had brought with them so many extremes, both good and bad. Her mind was now struggling to cope with anything else.

The bed dipped and then she was against Conner's warm chest, wrapped in his embrace.

"Shh, baby doll. I'll keep you safe. Robyn can't keep getting away with her actions. She'll slip up and get caught. You'll see."

"What about dad? He's the one she keeps going after."

"Jennifer will make sure he stays safe. Female shifters are just as protective as males. Your dad will be well protected so long as she's near, and by the look of them, she'll always be near until Robyn is caught."

She nuzzled her face against his mating mark, allowing the jolt of magic to help center her. "Can we just forget the whole thing? For today I just want to be normal. Go out and do something totally boring and human-like."

"Well, Kit and the team are still out at the Rally. We could head over and have lunch with them. Is that human and boring enough?"

She heard the humor laced in his voice and smiled against his flesh. "Yeah, not sure it will be at all boring, but it's definitely human enough for me."

He stroked her hair back from her face before cupping her jaw in his palm. His mouth descended on hers, devouring her as his fingers slid into her hair. He pulled back as her heart began to beat wildly. His forehead rested against hers.

"We'd better get moving then or we won't make it for lunch."

"Hmm, I suppose you've got a point. And, to be honest, I'm a little sore from all our nocturnal activities last night."

A frown creased his face. "I didn't hurt you did I?"

"Oh no, you didn't hurt me. You're just, well, rather large and my body is still getting used to your size. I'll be fine."

Her cheeks heated with a blush and she twisted her face away. With a finger beneath her chin, he turned her back to him and kissed her gently.

"You're so cute when you blush."

Before she could think of a response, he was up and striding toward the shower with her.

Chapter Twelve

Shivering, Robyn paced the small cabin. It had been three days since the incident at the lake and she'd not seen Barbara since. There was next to no food left in the kitchen and Robyn's mind kept running away with random thoughts. She now remembered the fresh damage on the front of Dale's car. Was Barbara responsible? Is that why she wasn't here?

She strode over to the sink and got herself a glass of water. With shaking fingers, she lifted the drink to her lips and sipped the cool liquid. Focusing on the feel of the soothing water going down her throat she managed to control the shivers wracking her body as she heard a car door close.

The squeak of the front door opening had Robyn gently placing the glass on the bench top. She looked up and caught Barbara's panicked expression.

"I can explain, Robyn."

"Explain what? Your absence? Or the damage to Dale's car?"

She felt her lips curl into a grin as Barbara's eyes peeled wide. "What? You didn't think I'd know about his car so soon?"

"I was doing what you asked!"

Rage rolled through Robyn. "I asked you to delay the others, not to injure Dale."

"I didn't injure him. I saw Jennifer sitting in the car and rammed into her, not him."

Robyn prowled around the bench, discreetly pulling a knife from the block on her way.

Barbara cocked an eyebrow at her before she backed away. Robyn guessed the look in her eyes must have given her intentions away.

"I'm sorry I was late but the cops hauled me in for the crash. I was charged, then released. They were following me everywhere! I couldn't come out here without leading the entire police force with me." She paused as her gaze dropped to the hand Robyn had behind her back. "What are you holding behind you, Robyn?"

With only a few steps now between them, Robyn was confident Barbara wouldn't be able to get away from her.

"A knife of course."

Robyn loved the way Barbara's eyes peeled wide with fear, the power that rushed through her veins as she quickly swiped the knife forward in an arc aimed at her throat. Barbara lifted her arm and the knife sliced deep into her forearm. Barbara's scream of pain stung her ears but it was too late now, Robyn was lost to the bloodlust. With no real thought to what she was doing, she reached for Barbara's arm and pulled it low as she stabbed forward with the knife, driving it deep into her chest straight into her heart.

"No one endangers what is mine. Dale is mine."

Robyn pulled the knife free and stepped back. Blood gushed rapidly from the wound. With a macabre fascination, she watched as Barbara slumped to the floor and a pool of blood grew around her. Her now pale skin stood out against all the red and Robyn saw the beauty in it. Robyn stayed there, fused to the spot as Barbara struggled with her final breaths. Once her chest ceased to move and her glassy eyes lay open and unblinking, Robyn snapped out of her trance and back to what she needed to do.

With no Barbara, she'd have to follow Dale herself. Good thing Barbara had come in a car. She bent forward and plucked the car keys from the pool of sticky blood. She calmly walked back to the kitchen where she used a paper towel to clean off the keys. She hoped the electronics in the locking mechanism still worked. Using another towel, she wiped off the knife before she strolled out of the cabin into the early morning light. She saw Barbara had brought Robyn's car and had left it conveniently sitting right out the front, which suited her just fine. She didn't need anyone catching a glimpse of her splattered in blood. They'd come to investigate and find the body.

Can't have the police getting involved before I get to Dale now can we?

She drove to Dale's rental place, where she very carefully parked far enough away that the patrol car that passed by every quarter of an hour didn't see her. As she waited for Dale to come out of his house and start his day, she noticed the damage to his car. His previously in-perfect-condition black Hilux was now sporting a serious dent and scrapes on the front passenger side. The scrapes were yellow. Barbara's car was yellow. The confirmation that Barbara was guilty of causing her man harm made her wish she could hurt the woman all over again.

"Such a pity."

After what felt like hours, Dale left his house. Robyn's hands gripped the steering wheel tight enough her knuckles turned white as Jennifer followed him out. Jennifer scanned the area as they hopped in the car and reversed out the drive.

"I will not be stupid. I will not be stupid."

She slowly started her car and followed at a safe distance as they left town.

They wound their way through the Tasmanian wilderness toward the coast. Where was he going? A sign on the road verge read 'Temporary Road Closures Ahead.' Ahh, of course, the International Bethotte Rally was on. He must be going somewhere to watch this leg of the race. Glancing at the clock, she noticed it was just past noon. Didn't they stop the race for a lunch break?

Dale turned into a track that was sign posted as an entry for rally volunteers. Robyn drove on until she found a small rest stop. Quickly parking, she palmed the knife she'd brought from the cabin and trekked to where Dale had turned off.

She slowed as she reached the pit-stop area. Tina and Conner were chatting with a couple of firefighters. So, they were all meeting up with Conner's work buddies for lunch. She kept far enough away to stay hidden—and down wind, she didn't want to risk those cat people sniffing her out—but close enough to catch the odd word spoken. Nothing useful. *Typical.* Then she heard Tina mention going to the toilet before she pushed away from the group.

Perfect.

Her chance had arrived.

Dale would never accept her so long as Tina was around to badmouth her. But if Tina were to have an accident, well, she couldn't whisper sweet nothings to her daddy dearest about Robyn now could she?

A flash of memory of Barbara lying in a pool of her own blood made her grin. *Wonder if Tina will look as pretty in red...* Clenching her grip on the handle of the large kitchen knife she made her way over to the transportable toilet block. She waited nearby for Tina to come out. Her legs began to tremble as nervous excitement bubbled through her. She liked the power killing brought on. Maybe once Tina was out of the way she could corner Jennifer...

Tina finally emerged from the building and as she did, Robyn pounced forward. Grabbing a fist full of Tina's hair she yanked with enough force to bring her wheelchair to a stop. Tina shrieked out briefly, but quickly silenced when Robyn pressed the blade against her throat.

"I'm done playing your games, Tina."

"I-I haven't been playing any game, Robyn."

The fear in Tina's voice fired her up. The thrill of the kill coursed through her veins.

"Oh but you have, convincing your father I'm not right for him. It's all your fault, you know? But once you're gone, he'll be mine."

She began to slide the knife across Tina's throat making a shallow slice, before she decided stabbing would be more fun. She pulled the blade away and pressed the tip to the side of Tina's pale neck. She paused a moment to observe the pulse fluttering furiously at the base of Tina's throat. Pressing in, Robyn enjoyed the feel of the blade as it slid through Tina's soft flesh.

Robyn cursed as Tina snapped from her frozen state and gripped Robyn's wrist tightly. Robyn laughed as this young girl thought she was stronger than her. Her laughter died suddenly when her hand spasmed and released the knife. Robyn watched in horror as Tina reached to grab the knife, which had fallen in front of her chair.

"I don't think so."

Robyn's grip had loosened on Tina's hair. She rectified that quickly. Again holding her immobile with her head pulled back, she watched the blood run down her neck from the open stab wound Robyn had left before losing the knife. Within moments the red liquid soaked Tina's shirt, sticking it to her skin. She could see the rapid rate of Tina's breathing. Tina tried to paw at her hand gripping her hair but very quickly it weakly fell away.

"Maybe I don't need to do anymore. I do believe I've done enough. There is a lot of blood and you are looking a little pale."

Robyn had wanted to watch Tina die as she held the knife deep within her flesh but the way Tina's eyes were now rolling back had Robyn buzzing with glee. Fear and pain etched deep into the creases of Tina's ever whitening face confirmed it wasn't worth Robyn loosening her grip to retrieve the knife that still lay at Tina's feet in the dirt. The risk of missing her last breath wasn't worth it.

Focused wholly on Tina, Robyn didn't hear anyone approach. A firm, tight grip around the wrist of the hand she had buried in Tina's hair was the first she knew they weren't alone. Robyn growled out her frustration as once again her hand slackened and released its hold. *Damn pressure points.*

"What the hell?"

Her arm was yanked away from Tina with such force her whole body spun around. She stumbled over some sticks and fell to her knees. Pain radiated up her legs, ripping an anguished cry from her throat. Fury clouded her vision as she cradled her injured wrist against her chest. She forced herself to focus, and raised her gaze to see who had derailed her plan.

The red haired woman from the hospital stood before

her in her yellow firefighters gear with fury written all over her perfect face.

"You piece of shit. I told you if you hurt her, I'd make you pay."

She watched, frozen, as the woman came forward and delivered an uppercut punch to beneath her jaw. She flew away from Tina and with a thud, hit the dirt. Agony radiated from her jaw and stars momentarily filled her vision before everything went black.

Conner roared as he felt Tina's pain and panic flare inside him. He spun and sprinted over to the toilet block. He skidded to a halt with his heart in his throat as he watched Kit deliver a knockout punch to a kneeling Robyn.

Damn it, the bitch got to Tina! Again!

He sprinted the remaining distance and dropped down in front of his mate. Her eyes were wide with obvious panic and alarm. Her hands were weakly attempting to grip her throat but all the blood had made her skin slippery. Her neck and chest were drenched in it. What had the bitch done?

"Oh damn baby, what did she do to you?"

His voice shocked him. It was so rough with his surging emotions. He knew she'd be lucky to hear him. He gently wiped his hands over her neck, quickly locating a stab wound that continued to pulse out blood. He quickly pressed his palm over the wound, applying pressure to stem the flow. Without moving that hand, he shifted the other to examine further. He wiped away blood to discover a shallow slice across her windpipe. White hot rage caused a shudder to run through him. Robyn had attempted to slice her throat! He would be eternally grateful that Kit had arrived when she had.

Focusing on what needed to be done, he made a quick assessment of her injuries. Both were covered up now, but it wasn't like he was going to forget what they looked like anytime soon. The stab wound would definitely need stitches but he was sure the cut on her throat would heal fine on its own. Now that they'd mated, she'd have slightly increased healing abilities. Not anywhere near what a full-blooded shifter had, but enough to fix that shallow cut, no problem. But that stab was a different story as was her blood loss.

He leaned in to press a kiss to Tina's cold lips before he quickly glanced around to check what was happening. He saw a man he didn't know tying up Robyn's wrists behind her back. She was out cold. Knowing how hard Kit could hit, especially when she was enraged, Robyn would be lucky if she woke up at all. Kit's voice caught his attention. She was on her radio calling for medic and police assistance. With that taken care of he turned his focus back to Tina. She stared blankly into his eyes. He could hear the shallowness of her breathing.

"Breathe, Tina. Nice deep breaths. You're going to be okay. Adele will come and fix you up. You'll be fine. Please, baby, breathe for me."

He watched as finally she took deeper inhales. She'd

been on the verge of passing out, he was sure. He could understand why she'd be more than a little panicked. She couldn't see her injury but had felt the knife slice her flesh. He'd probably be equally terrified in her position.

My poor mate must be petrified.

Dale appeared by Tina's side, dropped to his knees and kissed her cheek.

"I'm so sorry, sweet pea. This is all my fault."

Hearing her father take the blame channeled his anger to Dale. "Don't be daft, Dale. The blame for this is entirely on Robyn's head. You couldn't be expected to know how insane she was. Just be thankful we've finally caught the damn woman."

Conner's words brought a shudder from Dale as he closed his eyes and leaned against Tina. He saw the tears run down the tough man's face but didn't mention it. He could feel his own eyes sting with unshed tears at the thought of what could have easily happened here today.

"Owe you a drink or twenty, Kit."

"Nah, I got to take her out. That's reward in itself. Not that I'd turn down a free drink or two."

Kit gave his shoulder a squeeze and a low growl came from the man holding Robyn. With so many people and so much blood, it was impossible to scent one individual amongst the others, but Conner assumed the man was a shifter.

"Ah, Kit? What's the go with that?"

Desperate for a distraction before his tears broke through, he focused on his leap-sister.

"Ah, yeah. That would be rally driver, Jessie Lutrec. Apparently, he's my mate. Not sure he likes the idea, though."

"Why wouldn't he?"

Conner was confused. How could a shifter not be ecstatic about finding his mate?

"Because he doesn't understand. He's a new shifter, conceived with the last comet passing. I get the feeling he's never found another shifter until me."

Conner looked at Kit dumbfounded. If Jessie was a Comet Shifter and Kit's mate, that meant Kit was one too. Shit, she'd held that secret close to her chest. He'd always known Kit was a shifter, but not a Comet Shifter. Before he could ask any more questions, he was cut off by the sound of approaching sirens. He turned back to Tina. Unable to resist, he leaned in and kissed her cold lips, willing his warmth into her. He watched her eyes close and tears trickle down her pale cheeks.

"Shh, Tina. The ambulance's arrived now. You're safe. They're loading Robyn into the police wagon. She won't get bail again. You and your dad are safe."

Adele rushed over to them and stopped with a curse. "Bloody hell! What did the bitch do?"

Conner kept the pressure on Tina's wound as he helped Adele load her into the ambulance. With him beside Tina, Adele moved to close the doors. He heard Jennifer call out that she would drive Dale to the hospital.

He explained to Adele what had happened on the way.

The ride into town was blessedly short but still way too long for Conner's frayed nerves. Tina passed out as they entered the hospital. Conner kept the pressure on her wound until she was in emergency and Clint took over.

"This is going to take us a while, Conner. Why don't you head to an empty room and grab a shower. If we finish up before you're out, we'll come and get you."

Was Clint insane? No way would he leave his injured mate.

Adele's hand briefly rested on his arm. "Clint's right, *cher*. You're covered in blood and you know I won't leave her side until you return. I promise you, she will not be left alone for a second."

Conner looked down at his front to see that he was filthy. Blood, dirt and sweat had him looking terrible. Not wanting to freak out his mate when she woke, he nodded and headed toward the nurses' station to find out which room he could use.

A couple of minutes later he stood under the hot spray and watched as the red stained water flowed down the drain.

He was washing his mate's blood from his skin.

His precious mate had been injured. Again.

His body shuddered uncontrollably and he finally allowed his tears to flow freely. In the privacy of this locked bathroom he could give in to his emotions. He tilted his head back so the hot water struck his face, washing away his tears as they left his eyes. His emotions tangled and tightened. Fear for his mate, relief that Robyn was now caught, and shame that he hadn't protected Tina, all knotted together.

Going to the rally had been a bad idea. He should have realized with all the people milling around he'd never be able to smell if Robyn was close. Yet again, he'd misjudged a situation and his precious mate had paid the price. Scrubbing his face in his hands, he turned away from the spray. Taking a deep breath, he firmly pushed his emotions down. Tina needed him to be strong. Pumping some soap out of the wall dispenser, he quickly washed his body, rinsed and turned off the taps. He snagged one of the small scratchy hospital towels he'd brought in with him and dried off. With another tucked around his waist he headed out of the bathroom—hoping someone had brought him a change of clothes.

He opened the door to find Dominic leaning against the bed, arms folded over his broad chest. His brother's face was set in grim lines as he frowned at him.

"Hey Dom."

"Conner. Brought you some clothes and wanted to have a chat. Make sure you're doing okay."

Tears threatened again under the loving concern of his brother, but he held them back. Males didn't cry—and if they did it was in secret where no one could see. He distracted himself by focusing on getting dressed. His fingers stilled on the buttons as Dom broke the silence.

"Don't get caught up in the guilt, Conner. I know how you're feeling. I'll never be able to fully forgive myself for not checking the house before letting Kelly go back to her room that day."

Conner's gaze snapped up to his brother's. "But that's not your fault. How could you have known Cole was already inside the house?"

Dominic smiled sadly. "That's my point. I couldn't have known. Doesn't stop me constantly going over all the *if only*'s of it. *You* couldn't have known Robyn would be there today—or what she was going to do. All of us assumed she'd go after Dale, that's who we were watching. We *all* misjudged this one. Well, except for Kit."

"I should have been the one to save her. It should have been me to take the bitch out."

"Yeah, I get that. But you need to push aside your male ego and focus on the facts. Because of Kit, Tina is safe and Robyn's in custody. If she hadn't been there, and Tina had to wait for you to arrive…"

A shudder ran through him at Dom's unfinished sentence. "Yeah, I hear you. Tina would have been dead before I'd been able to reach her." He paused to sigh and scrub his face. "This whole having a mate thing is hell on your nerves isn't it?"

Dominic had the gall to laugh. "Yeah, it truly is. But it's worth every second." He slapped Conner on the back. "C'mon, let's get you to her side so you can stop fretting like a mother hen."

Conner punched Dom in the arm before he followed his still chuckling brother from the room to go find his mate.

He was sitting beside Tina, nuzzling into her cool palm when Dominic brought his parents, Dale and Jennifer into the hospital room. Thankfully it appeared everyone knew all that had happened as there were no questions of how. Conner couldn't bring himself to go over it again.

"Has she woken up yet?" His mother gently asked, as she eyed the bag hanging next to Tina.

"Not yet. That's her second bag of blood, she lost so much… Clint said she should wake up soon. All her vitals are looking good, aside from her low blood pressure."

"Have you completed the mating yet, son?"

A contented warmth spread through his chest at his father's quiet question.

"Yes, we completed it last night."

"Congratulations, and it means she'll heal more rapidly than she would have before. Not as fast as you do, though. Human mates have increased healing, but not to the full extent we do."

"I know, Dad. Dom and I do pay attention when you tell us stuff."

"Yeah well, a parent has to repeat things to make sure some days."

Adele shuffled into the room looking worn out. She headed straight over to Dom who scooped her up before he sat down with her nestled in his lap.

"You look beat, my sweet."

Adele nuzzled into Dom's neck. "I am, *mon amour*.

The fact I'm both a qualified nurse and paramedic meant I could stay with her the entire time."

Conner cleared his throat, feeling awkward as he attempted to express his gratitude.

"Ah, thanks, Adele. For staying with her. I felt better knowing family was in with her when I couldn't be."

Adele smiled over to him. "No problem, Conner. Tina's family. No way would I leave her."

Dale had been slowly creeping closer and closer to Tina. Conner suspected the scene was all a bit surreal to the poor man. They were used to shifters being real, but Dale no doubt was still coming to terms with it all. He reached her other side and lowered into a plastic chair. His hand slid beneath Tina's. He was obviously being careful to not disturb the tube in the back of her hand.

"Can someone explain what 'mating' is? I don't mean the how. That's just too much information for a father to hear about his daughter, but I want to know how it's changed her. Does she shift now?"

Conner was thankful when his dad stepped forward to answer Dale.

"She won't change from who she is, Dale. Being able to shift is in the DNA. You have to be born with it. When Tina mated with Conner, they bonded. Tina will be healthier now; she won't suffer from things like colds and flus. She will also heal faster than she did before. As a result, she will live longer. Most shifters live to over one hundred years. Their human mates are about the same."

Conner watched a frown descend over Dale's face before he turned to Jennifer who remained by the back wall, silently watching.

"I'm not your mate, am I?"

Jennifer moved forward toward Dale. "No, Ryan was my mate. Shifters only get the one. But as a Widow Mate I am able to find love again. Like humans, shifters are capable of loving more than one person."

She was now close enough to stroke Dale's face with her palm. She bent down to whisper in his ear and even though Conner couldn't hear what was said, the lines of worry smoothed from Dale's face and a small smile tugged at the edges of his lips. Dale turned into Jennifer and with his free hand, he gripped her jaw as he delivered a kiss which left his feelings for her clear for all present to see.

"Gah, Dad. Get a room."

Tina's groggy voice snapped Conner's attention straight to her pale face.

Tina couldn't help but smile at her father's blushing face. Her body felt heavy and she struggled to keep her eyes open, but seeing her Dad happy was worth the effort. So was seeing Conner. She rolled her head over to look at him. His face held worry lines and his eyes looked tired, but he was still the best looking man she'd ever seen. He had her hand against his cheek and he turned to press a kiss to her palm. She smiled at him.

"How are you feeling, baby doll?"

"I feel okay. Just really tired."

Conner nodded before he closed his eyes tightly. Tina knew he was feeling guilty over Robyn's attack.

"It's not your fault, Conner. Robyn made her choices."

In a fast movement, Conner had his face buried in her neck, and she could feel the hot splash as his tears hit her skin. She threaded her fingers into his hair and pressed a kiss to his head.

"I don't understand why she went for you, sweet pea. I thought she was only after me now that I was in town."

Grateful for the subject change her father offered, she looked at him to answer—being very careful to not move her bandaged neck. She knew Conner wouldn't want everyone to know he was crying. Her man was so tough on the outside, but on the inside he was a big soft kitten.

"She told me that so long as I was around I would prevent you from accepting her. In her deranged mind she thought if I were gone, she'd have you all to herself. I'm guessing Jennifer was next on her list."

She noticed Jennifer's hands tighten on her father's shoulders. Her dad responded by pressing a kiss to the top of one of her hands.

Looks like love is in the air for more than just Conner and me.

Conner's arm slipped around her waist and he pressed himself tighter into her. Tina cast Adele a quick look and she nodded in understanding.

"Well, I think Tina deserves a rest. How about we all

head off and give Conner and her a moment or two?"

Within minutes the door swung shut and they were alone.

"Conner? Are you all right?"

He wiped his face on the pillow before raising his head. His watery red rimmed eyes broke her heart.

"I'm just overwhelmed, I guess. I've never handled emotions real well, sweetheart, and today has been a damn roller coaster. I thought she'd taken you from me. I can't live without you Tina."

Before she could respond, he leaned in and kissed her. Both his palms cupped her face as he deepened the kiss. He pulled back a little and stared down at her, his gaze filled with his love for her. Her eyes became blurry and she blinked them clear. He wiped her tears with his thumbs.

"No more tears, baby doll. I can't handle it when you're upset."

"They're happy tears this time. I love you, Conner. More than I ever even dreamed possible."

Chapter Thirteen

Conner stood behind Tina with his hands gently resting on her shoulders and his body pressed against the back of her wheelchair. With her citrus scent floating up to him, he inhaled deeply then watched the others gather for the memorial service for Kelly's mother, who'd been murdered by Cole nine months ago. Adele was protectively curled around Kelly near the tombstone. Dominic stood close by, along with Adele's father. Remi and Choden stood beside Jake chatting quietly. They were waiting on the arrival of Kit and the others who had been working the rally. The sound of a loud bike brought all their attention to the car park. Kit on her baby, her red Ducati Monster 1100evo, pulled in followed by a couple of cars. He watched as his leap brothers and sister came forward to join them.

Choden moved to stand before the makeshift altar at the base of the grave. He helped a teary eyed Kelly light both the candles, safe from the breeze in hurricane glass style holders. They also lit the incense sticks that sat in front of a small stone Buddha. Adele stepped forward and gave Kelly a small bunch of white tulips. Her small sad voice cut through the silence, "I remember, back when I was little, when we were on the run from my father. For a treat Mum took us to a tulip farm. It's the only memory I have of Mum being happy. Smiling. So that's why I bought tulips today-" she broke off with a sob as she turned into Adele's embrace.

Choden chose that moment to begin chanting. The sounds of the ancient Tibetan prayer soothed Conner's heart. He hoped it did the same for poor little Kelly. She'd been through so much in her short life. Hopefully being able to say goodbye to her mother would help her move forward so she could heal and begin living. To start things off, Conner wheeled Tina forward and they both put their single red tulip blooms next to Kelly's white ones. As he wheeled her back, the others stepped forward to place their flowers. By the time everyone had filed past the grave, it was covered in a rainbow of tulips. Surely wherever Kelly's mum was, she'd be able to see this and be both proud of and happy for her daughter.

Just as Choden began to conduct the memorial service, Conner noticed Remi sharply turn his head away from grave and toward a stand of trees. Conner saw his nose flare and heard the low growl he made. Taking a deep breath himself, he caught a scent of a human female. It was familiar but he couldn't place it. Remi said something to Dominic before moving toward the trees. With a nod of his head, Dominic indicated Conner should follow. Conner bent forward to kiss Tina's cheek. "I'll be back in a bit, baby doll. Don't stray from Kit's side while I'm gone, okay? Barbara is still out there somewhere."

Tina nodded and the tear that slid down her cheek tore at his heart. He didn't want to leave her here without him, but he had to deal with what might be a potential threat against her, or some other member of his leap. He would not fail her again.

"I'll be back as soon as I can. I promise."

With a last quick kiss to her soft skin, he jogged after Remi.

As he reached the trees, he heard Remi growl low and quiet. Never a good thing with a shifter.

"Who are you?"

A woman's choked sob was the only response Remi received. Conner rushed past a large gum tree and froze to the spot. Remi had the woman pinned from behind in a bear hug grip, his nose pressed to her neck as the woman shuddered in his arms. Conner looked at the woman. Really looked at her. It had to be Gloria. She looked too similar to Tina to be anyone else.

"Are you Barbara?"

Remi's question brought another sob from the woman, in a shaky voice she murmured. "No. Not Barbara. Gloria, my name is Gloria."

Conner moved forward as he spoke. "She's Tina's mother, Remi."

Remi released her so fast she stumbled forward, landing on the ground on all fours. Conner stepped up close to her and offered a hand to help her up. As she rose, Remi's questions continued.

"If you are Tina's mother, why are you here hiding?"

Conner's body was tense. This was the woman who had caused his mate so much pain by abandoning her. But without all the events happening just as they had, Tina wouldn't have been in Rosebery. She wouldn't be with him yet. He would have found her eventually of course, but Gloria's actions had hastened the process for which Conner was grateful.

"She's hiding, Remi, because she hurt her daughter. This *devoted* mother decided that once Tina was injured she was no longer worthy to be in her care. Isn't that right, Gloria? You knew Tina's days at competition level gymnastics were over and with it, your days of being able to bask in the glory of being the mother of a top athlete."

He watched as Gloria's eyes filled with more tears and her lower lip trembled. He almost felt sorry for her. But he wouldn't let his guard down until he knew why she was here, stalking Tina. He'd already failed his mate enough times. No one else would hurt her on his watch.

"Why are you here, Gloria?"

With a deep breath, she stiffened her shoulders. "I'm here to speak with my daughter. My reasons are none of your concern."

"Your reasons are very much my concern. Tina is my fiancé. I refuse to allow you to hurt her again."

With eyes wide in obvious shock, she covered her mouth with her hand. "Tina's engaged? She didn't tell me." Conner watched her pause to shake her head slightly as she closed her eyes briefly. "Of course she didn't. Look, I made a mistake. Several mistakes. I'm here to try to fix them, not to cause my daughter any more grief."

Conner wasn't sure what to do. He didn't have a problem with Gloria seeing Tina if she truly wanted to apologize, but in the middle of the memorial service was not the time or the place. Remi stepped in and handed Gloria a small packet of tissues he'd had in his back pocket.

"How about I take Gloria over to the Top Pub? She can speak with Tina after the service. I don't think her attending the memorial is the way to go."

"Good idea, Remi. I agree, now is not the time. I'll let Dom and Adele know what's happening. We'll see you both over there a bit later. And Gloria? Your intentions better be pure. I will not stand for Tina being hurt again. Do you understand me?"

She gave him a shaky nod and Remi took her elbow to lead her away. Conner stood still, hands on his hips as he watched them walk toward the car park. Remi was standing closer than necessary. His posture looked protective, almost possessive. Remi's mate, Adele's mother, had died years ago, so he was free to find love again. He'd been told it wasn't as intense as the mating bond but it was still strong.

Remi deserved to find love again, but Conner wasn't sure Gloria was the right choice. She'd hurt so many who had loved her.

Remi had lost his mate when he was still a teenager. He'd impregnated Fleur with Adele, and her parents freaked out and sent her from France to Australia to live. Remi had then spent over twenty years searching for them. Sadly, he didn't find them until after Fleur had died from cancer. It was only because of all the trauma of being kidnapped by Cole, then bonding with Dom in their mating, which set off the dormant shifter genes in Adele that she was found at all. They had all assumed Adele was fully human, but after mating with Dom she'd shifted and their dad had done some fast research into her background.

Shaking himself free from his internal musings, he headed back to the others. He strode over to his dad who was now standing near Dominic and quickly explained what had happened.

"That's interesting. You intend to warn Dale before we head over there? Not sure he'd like that kind of surprise."

"Yeah, not sure I'm looking forward to this showdown."

Conner moved back over to Tina. He hated being away from her, especially when she was upset. He ran his hand through her hair, massaging her scalp a little with his strong fingers. She leaned into his touch with a small sigh. Choden's strong voice chanting brought his attention back to the ceremony which was just finishing up. He focused on the Tibetan words, allowing the sounds to soothe and calm him once again. It was going to be a long afternoon and he was going to need all the patience he could muster.

🎩

Tina allowed Conner to push her up the ramp at the back entrance to the Top Pub. Her mother was inside waiting. Rubbing the back of her neck, she had the sudden urge to run away.

"I can't do this, Conner. Take me home. Just-"

"Shh, Tina. It's going to be fine." He knelt down beside her chair and took her face in his palms. "Both our dads and I are going to be there. Dominic and the other cats will be close by. She won't hurt you."

Tina loved Conner's protectiveness, even when he went overboard. She couldn't understand his guilt over not being able to protect her from Robyn. It wasn't his fault and she didn't blame him any more than she blamed her dad, but he wasn't ready to hear it yet.

"Conner, Mother has never physically hurt me. She does all her damage with her tongue or by leaving."

"She told Remi and me that she'd made mistakes, that she was here to make them right. All we can do is give her a chance to say what she's come to say. If you still don't want her to be part of your life after that, it's your call. I don't want to push you, but I think you'll regret it if you don't hear her out. I'll support whatever you decide."

Taking a deep breath, Tina wet her lips. "Okay, well let's just rip this Band-Aid off then. C'mon."

She started to push herself forward, and Conner

proved he was learning her moods as he let her enter the private dining room under her own steam. She had to meet Gloria on her own terms. She needed to be strong, and being able to push herself into that room was a great start to keeping up that appearance. She didn't need her mother's approval. It was all a mask, but her mother didn't know that.

Once inside the door, she surveyed the room. Adele's father, Remi was it, stood with his arms crossed over his broad chest in the shadows. His hard gaze was focused solely on the woman nervously pacing the length of the room. As her mother hadn't noticed her, she took a moment to watch. Her head was down. Her clothes were as perfect as always, but her shoulders were curled forward a little. She wrung her hands in front of her. The door closed behind Conner, and Gloria's head snapped up as her feet ground to a halt. Tina sucked in a shocked breath. Her mother's eyes showed pain and there were dark smudges beneath them, dark enough to be visible through her makeup.

"Tina."

The way her mother said her name made her knees weak. It was filled with anguish. Could her mother really be sorry? If she was, what the hell had happened to cause it?

"Hello Mother. Why are you here?"

Tina was so on edge. Seeing Gloria brought back all the feelings of rejection like it happened yesterday.

"I'm here to apologize. I'm hoping you'll forgive me

and give me another chance to be part of your life.”

“No offence, but I can’t recall a time you ever apologized for anything. What happened? Something had to have happened to trigger this.”

Gloria started pacing again as she drove her fingers into her hair, messing the perfectly styled tresses.

“I’ve been so selfish. I didn’t even see what I was doing. It would be easy to blame how I was raised… My parents always instilled in me how important appearances were. To always make sure you had the best, no matter the cost.” She paused to crumple down into a chair before raking her hair again. “I always did my best to please them. Did everything they wanted me to do. Even after they both passed, I still tried.”

So far, her mother hadn’t told her anything new. Tina had worked out long ago how vain and self-centered her maternal grandparents were.

“They passed years ago, Mother. That doesn’t explain what’s made you suddenly change your tune now.”

“I was just trying to explain why I did what I did. I know there is no excuse, Tina. I abandoned you when you needed me the most. I get that now. After Dale came and took you I instantly felt your loss. The house was hollow, just a shell without life. Then I went to a couple of dinner parties and other functions. But again it just seemed empty. Without you I had nothing to live for. I do love you, Tina. I may not have always shown it as I should have, but I have always loved you. Then word got out about what I’d done. I was very quickly shunned. In a matter of days I realized I had no real friends. Then, my boss at David Jones called me in and told me straight out that I needed to see what was in front of me. He told me how he always put work before his family and now his kids are grown and he rarely sees them because he never bothered to build a relationship with them.

"I had a lot of time on my hands to think over everything. As I looked back over my life, I realized how much of it I've wasted with superficial garbage. How many good people I've hurt." Her mother looked over her shoulder and her eyes filled with tears. Tina guessed her dad had joined them at some point. She was proved right when, with a slight croak in her voice, Gloria continued, "You two were hurt worst. Dale, Tina? Can you forgive me? I know I can't turn back time to fix it, but will you let me try to fix it now?"

Her father stepped in front of her, brushing a loving hand over her hair on his way past. "Gloria, words are not going to cut it for either of us. You'll need to hang around and prove you mean it."

"That's my intention. I've quit my job and have movers bringing all my things down-"

Her dad cut Gloria short. "Some things will never be as they were again though, you understand that, right? I've moved on. I have a woman in my life now. We might only be just starting out, but it's good. I'm not throwing that away because you want to relive the *good ol' days*. Not happening."

"Oh, Dale that was never what I meant. I never

expected to stroll into town and for us to simply pick up being a family again. I caused you so much pain, I am truly sorry. I will prove it to you. Our relationship will be vastly different in the future. I will never come between you and any woman you have. I simply want to be a part of Tina's life and for us to be civil to each other. I want to build myself a life here in Rosebery. A real life."

Tina sat silently, observing her parents interact with each other. She was feeling lightheaded, probably due to the shock of her mother's declaration. Could she trust Gloria? Did she really want to change into someone more, well, human? She'd already been thinking about past occasions with new eyes. Seeing things she hadn't before. Letting her mother back into her life would be a risk. But would it be worth it? Conner's hands moved over her shoulders where they squeezed before rising to massage her neck. His cedarwood and sage scent enveloped her and gave her added strength. No matter what happened with her parents, she would always have Conner. That thought reassured her as Gloria finished talking with her dad and turned to her with clear expectation in her gaze.

"I can't just forgive and forget, mother. I need time to, adjust, I guess, and to see if you are for real. Like the saying goes, *actions speak louder than words*. I need to see if your actions are going to match your words."

The tear that spilled down her mother's cheek as she nodded cracked her heart but Tina didn't budge. Gloria had to earn her place in Tina's life, if that's what she wanted. Tina would never live the shallow, materialistic lifestyle her mother had lived for so long. No way in hell. She preferred her life now. She might not be competing, which she had loved, but she had a really well rounded life now. That included true friends and a fiancé. A handsome sexy wonderful *mate* who would always be by her side.

"I think we've spent enough time away from everyone else. We're here to help Kelly grieve and celebrate her mother's life. Not drag our crap into it. So, let's all be mature adults and go out and join our family?"

Conner pressed a kiss to her head and whispered. "Well done," as he pulled her chair toward the door.

"Wait! Tina, I will prove it to you. I promise. I mean what I say, and congratulations on your engagement. Conner seems like he's perfect for you."

How did she know Conner's name? Oh, of course, they met at the cemetery. "Thanks, Mother. He is perfect and he makes me happier than I've ever been."

As Conner took her from the room, followed closely by her dad, she caught a glimpse of Remi moving to comfort her mother who remained sitting down. *Interesting.* But something that could wait for another day. Today was all about Kelly and her moving forward.

Conner sprinted through the bush, reveling in the feel of the twigs and branches that brushed against him. Splashing through a stream, he made his way deeper into the Cradle Mountain National Park, far from where any stray hiker might accidentally catch a glimpse of him.

Reaching a small clearing, he stood looking up to the sky, allowing the sun to warm him. He hadn't gone for a run in his snow leopard form in so long. With everything that had been happening, he'd needed it desperately.

What did you stop for?

Dominic's voice floated through his mind. They couldn't talk as leopards, but they could speak into each other's minds. They could also feel each other's emotions, so Dominic knew full well why Conner had stopped.

Just enjoying the sunshine on my fur for a bit.

I figured you must have stopped for a breather, since you haven't been for a run in so long. You probably need a break every so often now.

There was a heavy dose of humor in his brother's voice, but it didn't prevent Conner's answering growl or him chasing after his older sibling. They ran for a good half hour before Conner caught up to Dominic. Wrestling him to the ground, he stood above him, watching his brother pant.

Now who's out of practice? Mated life slowing you down, bro?

A heartbeat later, Conner was on the ground with his brother's jaws wrapped gently around his throat.

Careful there, Conner. You shouldn't tempt me to prove just how strong I am now that I'm fully mated.

You feel it too?

Dominic released him and lay down in a ray of

sunshine. No matter how old they were, they'd always have an inner kitten. Conner cocked his head in humor as Dominic squirmed on his back, sunning his underside. Once he found the perfect spot, he responded to his question.

Feel what?

Stronger. Since mating, I've noticed I'm stronger. All my skills are amplified. Dad never told us about that side of it.

Yeah, mating amplifies things all right. Dad never told us, because the Council of Alphas decided eons ago that it was something we didn't need to know until after we'd mated. Kind of like a surprise mating gift.

Pretty cool gift.

They both lay in silence for a few moments, enjoying the sun and fresh air, but Conner could sense something was weighing on his brother.

I can sense you're churning over something, Dom. Spit it out already.

How'd that meeting with Gloria go?

You mean what did she want.

Well, yeah, that too.

Apparently she's seen the light and wants to fix the relationships in her life. Guess we'll just have to wait and see if her actions support her words.

Well, if she does anything out of line with what she's saying, we'll know about it. Remi's keeping a close watch on her for us.

Conner shook his head. *I don't think Remi's watching*

her for our benefit, Dom.

Yeah, I did notice he's paying a lot of attention to her. Just hope she doesn't rip his heart out too.

Oh well, not much we can do about it at this point. Let's head back, we've been away for too long.

Yeah, with Robyn caught I doubt Barbara will try anything but still…

My feelings too. Adele is a lot stronger now, and if someone threatened any of them she'd shift and be able to protect them. But I'd still prefer to be there.

With a burst of movement, Conner rolled to his feet.

Race you back.

Dom's laugh echoed through his mind as he leapt through the scrub back to his mate.

It didn't take more than a quarter of an hour to return. They had instinctively worked a big circle around their females as they ran and played with each other. Conner burst through the bush into the clearing, sure he'd beaten his brother. A low growl was all his warning before his brother pinned him to the ground with a thump.

Damn, Dom. Do you have to pull this shit in front of my mate?

Of course I do, why do you think I did it? My mate's watching too.

Conner lunged at his brother and continued their play fight. They were both purring loudly so their mates and Kelly would know they were only playing.

"You boys cut it out already. I swear, human or animal, boys never grow up."

"Preaching to the choir here, Adele."

Kelly's laugh filled the air as she ran over to Dominic. Conner padded over to Tina where he curled around her on the picnic rug and watched as Dominic crouched low to allow Kelly to hop on his back. She grabbed fists full of fur and squealed when Dominic began moving. He took Kelly on a ride through the nearby bush, never leaving their sight as he slowly increased his speed.

Tina turned and buried her face and hands into the fur of his neck.

"Hmmm, you're so soft."

He preened under her compliment and purred loudly as he delivered a lick up her cheek. She laughed loud with her head thrown back. Conner loved seeing her like this. Completely carefree and happy. She would be like this every day of their lives if he had anything to do with it.

"That was so much fun!"

Kelly's excited voice pulled his attention from Tina to her. Dominic crouched down again and she climbed off and ran straight to Adele with the biggest grin Conner had ever seen the kid have.

"Well, now you're all back, how about you boys change so we can eat our lunch?"

Conner reluctantly moved to his feet, nuzzling his head into Tina's embrace before he trotted over to the large gum they had left their clothes behind. He watched as a blue glow enveloped Dominic before he began his own shift.

"You know Kelly's going to want to do that all the time, right?"

Dominic chuckled. "Probably. I don't mind. It's fun having her laughing her heart out while I race around with her on my back."

They finished dressing in silence while Conner shored up his courage.

"Dom? What's being a father like?"

"Why? You got Tina pregnant already?"

"No, well, at least, not that I know about. I was just thinking. That's all."

"Conner, you'll be a great dad. Don't worry about it. I'm guessing it's different with Kelly, because she's older and has issues from her past. But fatherhood is mostly an instinct thing. You need to follow what you feel is right—and listen to your mate. Adele just knows things I'd never thought about. C'mon let's go eat, maybe a full stomach will stop you going all girly on me."

Conner growled but didn't move toward his brother. Dominic seemed to be getting way too much enjoyment out of riling him up lately. Maybe Mum was right and if he started ignoring him, Dom'd give him a break. Conner seriously doubted Dom would ever stop, but it was worth a shot.

Seeing Tina happily chatting with Adele and Kelly had his heart swelling. She was so beautiful sitting there on the picnic rug, with the sun shining off her hair. It kind of looked like she had a halo glowing above her white-blond tresses. She looked up at him with a sparkle in her eye as he reached her side. Unable to resist, he dropped down and gave her a solid kiss, only pulling away when Kelly started making gagging noises at them. *Kids.*

His phone began ringing as the women started serving up lunch. Pulling it free, he checked the caller ID. Damn, it was a private number. Moving away from everyone to the other side of the clearing, he answered the call.

"Hello, Conner White here."

"Mr White, this is Detective Ross from the Rosebery Police."

Oh shit, what the hell had happened now?

"What's happened? Please don't tell me Robyn has escaped custody."

"No, nothing like that. Robyn is still in her cell I assure you. I'm ringing in regard to Barbara Johnson."

At the mere mention of her name his whole body tensed, Conner knew this wasn't going to be pretty.

"What about her?"

"She's been located. You know that small tourist park down Murchison Highway?"

"Yeah, sure. It's real small. Only has a couple of cabins and a stack of unpowered campsites."

"Well, it appears she was assisting Robyn, hiding her in one of those cabins. Our guess is something happened to make Robyn turn on her."

"Are you saying she's dead?"

"That's exactly what I'm saying. And I can tell you it

was not pretty."

"So, Tina and Dale are finally safe now?"

"I believe so. With Barbara dead and Robyn locked up, neither poses a risk to them."

"Where are things with Robyn? She's not going to get bail again is she?"

"No. Definitely not getting bail after she jumped it last time. To be honest, I doubt she'll make it to a hearing. She's gotten worse since her arrest. She is being assessed this afternoon and my guess is she'll be institutionalized for the rest of her life."

"Good, that's good. Look, I have to run but thanks for the call. You'll keep me posted about what happens with Robyn?"

"Yeah, I can do that for you. Have a good one."

He hung up his phone and scrubbed his face with his hands as relief poured through his body.

The threat to Tina was over.

He returned to the others and scooped Tina up so he could hold her close. His body shuddered as elation coursed through him. His mate was safe.

"You going to tell us what that call was about? Maybe loosen your grip so your mate can breathe again…not that pale blue doesn't suit her…"

Dom's words snapped him free from his introspection and he lowered down onto the rug with Tina now loosely held in his lap.

"Sorry, baby doll. I didn't hurt you, did I?"

She laid the sweetest kiss on his cheek. "Not at all.

Your brother was stirring you up again. Who was on the phone?"

Conner proceeded to give them all a recap of the phone call. He was careful to only allude to Barbara's death. Kelly didn't need to hear about more death so close to burying her mother.

Chapter Fourteen

Gripping the two Lofstrand crutches in her hands, Tina pushed down the nausea and slowly walked across the floor of the rehab room at the hospital. Clenching her jaw, she ignored the sweat trickling down her back. Finally she was walking and she wasn't going to let some stomach bug hold her back. Conner had told her now that they were bonded she shouldn't get sick but she was definitely coming down with something.

She made it to the far wall and turned to grin at Nina. She'd done it.

For the first time without falling, she'd made it the whole way across the room.

"I did it!"

"You sure did, Tina. Well done."

"Do you think I'll be able to walk down the aisle?"

Nina smiled gently. "I'm sure you will. It might be with a crutch or two, but you'll get down that aisle on your own two feet. However, that's enough for today. You don't want to push too hard and hurt yourself."

Tina leaned against the wall as Nina came over with her chair. Sinking down into it, she gasped as her legs throbbed. Apparently taking the weight off them was like a neon sign alerting her legs that it was okay to hurt, and of course that set her tummy off. Somehow she managed to convince her stomach to keep its contents

With her tummy slightly settled, she leaned forward to rub her legs and a twinge in her neck brought her hand to the small scar on side of her throat. It had been two weeks since Robyn had attacked her. Her wound healed up a lot faster than she'd expected. Conner had told her along with not getting sick she would heal faster—at least the faster healing part of things seemed to be working. However, when she tensed her muscles for a long period of time—like she did with rehab—it would quite often spasm. Clint told her it would stop on its own in time. She shuddered as she remembered the attack. Without Kit's help, Robyn would have no doubt done a hell of a lot more damage. Thankfully this time Robyn's bail was refused. She was currently being securely held in a psychiatric hospital far away from Rosebery.

"So, when is the big day again?"

Nina's question snapped her out of her memories.

"Christmas Day."

"Wow, seven weeks to organize it all. You sure you're going to be ready?"

"Oh, it'll all be perfect. Neither Conner nor I want a big fancy wedding, and all our family will be in town already so we figured we'd do it all together. Adele, Sophie and Kelly are all more than happy to help me organize everything. I guess Mother might want to help too."

Not that Tina wanted her to. Tina knew no matter how much of a changed woman Gloria was, she still had no idea what 'low key' meant.

The wedding didn't scare Tina at all. Not the organizing or the fact she was making a commitment to Conner. No, it was what was going to happen after the wedding that left Tina feeling a little lost. She had always been an athlete. That took up most of her time and energy. She'd never thought about doing anything else. Now she had her whole life ahead of her and no real idea what she was going to do with it. She knew she couldn't just sit at home waiting for Conner to return from work. She just wasn't wired that way. As much as she missed the actual gymnastics, now that she had real friends in her life, she didn't miss all the superficiality of high level athletics. Maybe that's why her stomach was playing up? Could it be because she was so stressed?

"Well, it sounds lovely. And speaking of your man, looks like he's here to whisk you away."

She sat up straight in her chair, turning a pleading look at Nina. "Oh, please don't tell him I'm walking yet. I want to surprise him at the wedding."

Nina's face broke out into a huge grin. "That's a great idea. You're going to shock the socks off him when he sees you do it."

"Thanks, Nina."

With Nina holding the door open, Tina wheeled out to where Conner stood waiting for her. He leaned down to give her a quick but passionate kiss before he pushed her out to his car.

"How'd it go, baby doll? You're looking a little pale, your stomach still giving you trouble?"

"My tummy's still a little cranky, but I'm thinking it might just be stress. It'll be fine soon I'm sure. The rehab is coming along really well...But I'm desperately in need of a shower."

He chuckled at her. "Well, yeah, I wasn't going to say anything but you're rather sweaty."

"Gee, thanks. Are you telling me I stink?" Humor laced her voice. Conner could be so damn cheeky.

"Never would I do such a thing. I'm wounded you would think that of me." He said in mock horror. With a wink, he continued. "C'mon, let's get home where I can make sure you're all clean."

She allowed him to lift her into the car and as she buckled herself in, he packed up her chair and jumped in the driver's side. As they drove out of the car park, her thoughts turned to her future.

"Are you sure you're okay? You're not in pain, are you?"

"No, I'm fine. Well, my legs and neck ache a little, and my tummy's not overly happy with me, but nothing major. Why?"

"Because you've got a nasty looking frown happening. What's up?"

"Oh, I've just been thinking about my future."

"Ah, hence the stress. Is it looking that bad? I thought I was a good catch."

She could hear the humor in his voice, and she appreciated his effort to cheer her up.

"Oh, you're definitely a great catch, honey. I mean with my career. I've only ever been an athlete, and that's not ever going to be possible again. I can't just sit around all day, every day. It will drive me nuts."

"Funny you should say that. I was chatting with Mum this morning when an idea occurred to me. You like working with numbers right?"

"Yeah, I've always been good at math. What are you thinking?"

"I was thinking you could have a go at accounting at Uni. You know, only if you wanted to."

Tina leaned back against the seat. Accounting. Suddenly she couldn't work out why she hadn't already thought of it.

"That's definitely something to consider, but I need something physical too. I don't ever want to get into the high level stuff again, but I want to keep my strength and fitness up. That is, once this rehab is over and I get back to normal."

"Actually, Adele suggested something a while back in that regard. I wasn't going to say anything until your rehab was further along."

"What idea is that?"

"You could teach. Just because you can't compete in gymnastics doesn't change how much you know about it. You could teach classes or coach individuals. There is a club here in town. I'm sure they'd love to have someone with your knowledge and expertise on board."

Tina's head jerked back as she blinked in surprise. "I suddenly feel really stupid for not seeing that as an option. How could I have not thought of that? Or the accounting thing."

"Well, in your defense. You've been more than a little busy."

She chuckled. "Yes, there's nothing quite like a crazy woman coming after you to keep you distracted."

Looking out the windshield, she smiled as their house came into view.

"Home sweet home."

The car slowed to a stop and Conner's finger beneath her jaw turned her face toward him so his lips could take hers with a heated passion she felt all the way to her toes.

"I love you, Tina."

"And I you."

Tina felt lighter as Conner pulled back from her to hop out. She could go to university, teach others at the gym then come home to her man. There was a good chance her life might have a 'happily ever after' included in it after all.

Conner opened her door and scooped her up in his arms. "I do believe I owe you a shower, my love."

"Yes, I do vaguely recall you mentioning it earlier."

Not bothering with her chair, Conner took her inside the house. The whole way she focused her attention on the sweet spot at the junction of his neck and shoulder, before nibbling her way up his throat. With a groan, he all but ran through the house to the bathroom with her giggling the entire way.

Life really was good.

Conner pushed open the front door and called out. His dad answered from the direction of his office so Conner headed that way, snagging a coffee on his way through the kitchen.

"Hey Dad- oh hi Dom, didn't know you were here too."

"Hi Conner, yeah, just catching up on Leap stuff with Dad."

"Hi son, what brings you over today? Tina let you off your leash?"

Dom roared a laugh. "Or you let her out of bed finally?"

Conner felt the heat of a blush stain his cheeks and he glared hard at his brother. "Piss off, Dom. I'm newly mated and have been off rotation at the station. You're no different with Adele." He moved his focus back to his dad as he cleared his throat. "Tina's gone dress shopping with Gloria. To be honest, I'm a little nervous about the whole thing. I thought if I was here you two can stop me from stalking them the entire time."

His dad shook his head as he chuckled. "Oh to be newly mated. Tina will be fine I'm sure. After everything her mother has done to her over the years, I think you should be more worried about what Tina will do to Gloria, rather than the other way around."

"Nah, Gloria's safe. Remi's following them."

All three of them chuckled at Conner's statement.

"It seems Remi has become quite smitten with Gloria. So far, Gloria seems to be living up to her claims of wanting to be a better person. I hope it works out. Remi could certainly use some happiness in the romance department."

"You got that right Dad. Remi loves spending time with us, getting to know his daughter. But he needs more in his life. Hopefully Gloria can step up."

"Yeah, hopefully. What were you two talking about before I came in? I need distracting, remember?"

"We were beginning to make plans for a Search. We need to locate more lost ones, including our comet shifters. They turned fifteen eleven years ago. That's a long time to be left out in the world alone."

"Kit and Jessie aren't ours?" Conner had always assumed Kit was Aussie.

"No, Conner. Kit's parents migrated from South America when she was small. Not sure what country. Jessie is the reason we're pushing up the search. He is a classic example of what can happen if a shifter isn't with other shifters. No one has ever educated him on any part of being a shifter. Kit's going to have her hands full for a long time. I'm just grateful that as a rally driver he travels all over and ended up here in Tassie."

"So who are you thinking of sending?"

"Xander will definitely head off. He'll lead the search. I was hoping the twins would join him. The three of them should be able to get the job done without alerting Trigger to what they are. I don't want to send out a massive group of men. That would just draw more attention than we want."

Conner totally agreed with his Dad on that one. Trigger was a nasty group that hunted shifters to kill them. So far, they hadn't found their leap here in Tasmania. They'd all like to keep it that way.

"Where are they focusing on?"

Dominic stepped forward, pointing to a map of the whole of Australia that was spread out on the desk. "That's what we were discussing when you came in, little brother. The logical place to start is Victoria, head up through New South Wales onto Queensland before heading west through Northern Territory to Western Australia. Then down the coast and over east again to South Australia. Then back to Victoria to come home on the ferry. They will hook up with leaps as they go, to take on the care and training of any shifters they find."

"Just thinking out loud, but since they're touring all the leaps anyway, why don't we get the boys to take photos of all the unmated females? Make it easier for at least some of our males to find their mates."

"Not a bad idea, Conner. The women would have to give their permission of course. And we can't let it turn into a dating service. Maybe if just the alphas of the leaps have access…"

"We're going to need to send out a letter or email to each leap explaining about the Search. We might as well include this idea in with it. See what the reaction is from the leaps."

Conner grinned as his father and brother continued to discuss his idea. The alpha and future alpha of the Australian Continental Leap had listened to and liked his idea. Even though they were his family, they didn't have to take notice of him. It was a great feeling. He also realized how childish he'd been to be jealous of his brother. Sure, he would never be the alpha like Dominic was destined to be, but he had his place in the leap too. His brother and father would always hear him out if he had suggestions, and they always respected him and his opinion—as they did every member of the leap. He guessed he could thank the fact he was now mated. It had mellowed him out enough that he could sit back and see what was right in front of him. Something he was beyond grateful of. His life felt complete. Well, nearly complete. When he and Tina had kids—then his life would be whole.

Tina wiped her palms down her thighs. She was so nervous, and the butterflies were not helping her stomach one bit. So far her mother had done all the right things but this was the test. A whole day with her shopping for wedding things. Would Gloria be able to accept that Tina wanted a simple gown? The wedding was going to be low key, elegant and private with just family and close friends. Tina most definitely didn't want to resemble a cream puff on her trip down the aisle. She chuckled quietly.

Conner won't know whether to eat me or marry me.

"Good morning, Tina, such a beautiful day. Early summer in Tasmania is always a lovely time of year."

"Yeah, it is a nice day. I'm glad you could make it."

Tina was sure her nerves showed through in her tone but her mother had sounded equally nervous so maybe she didn't notice Tina's.

"Of course I made it! This is your wedding dress we're buying. This is a vital mother-daughter shopping experience. And I was also hoping we could maybe chat a little over the day."

"Of course we will, Mother. How about you sit down and we start with a coffee before we hit the shops."

"You know, *Mother* sounds so formal. I want our relationship to be more intimate than what it was before. Would you be comfortable calling me Mum?"

Tina grinned a true smile. She'd always hated the whole 'mother' thing, made her feel like she was back in the 1800s."I'd like a closer relationship too, Mum."

"Okay, let's have that coffee. How do you have yours these days, Tina?"

"Same as always, white with one. Thanks, Mum."

Gloria headed in to order their drinks and Tina smiled as she watched. Her thoughts had scattered with the 'call me mum' comment.

Minutes later they both sat sipping at their coffees.

"So, Tina, do you have any ideas about what you want for your wedding dress?"

"I have a few ideas. Even though it's the middle of summer I want a long dress, I don't want anyone seeing my scars. I want it simple, nothing over the top with frills and lace. I don't want a train either. That will get caught up in my crutches."

Her mum grinned broadly at her. She'd told her about her plan of walking down the aisle as a surprise.

"I can't wait to see Conner's face when you walk to him. So, have you looked at pictures? Do you want straps?"

"I've had a bit of a look, but I haven't been feeling that well this last week so haven't bought magazines like I wanted too."

"Oh, honey, why didn't you call me? I'd have brought some around to you."

She gave her mum a sheepish smile. "Guess I just didn't think of that."

Tina started fidgeting under her mother's sudden intense scrutiny. "What? Have I got food stuck between my teeth or something?"

"Your teeth are fine, but you are looking, well, to be honest, glowy. How sick have you been feeling?"

"Oh you know. The usual, I'm really tired—but I've been pushing hard at rehab—so it takes me a while to get going in the morning. I'm off my favorite foods…"

Tina let the words hang in the air as realization dawned. "Oh my-bloody hell. I'm pregnant aren't I?"

Her mum's smile was a true smile, her eyes glittering in the sunlight. "Well, it would be wise to take a test but

I'm guessing that's what has you feeling ill."

"Well, I guess a trip to the pharmacy is added to our places to go today."

"I think that would be a good idea. Tina, I have to ask you this and please don't take me the wrong way. As your mother I need to make sure. Are you happy? I mean this has all happened very fast."

Tina felt a warmth spread through her, at both her mother caring enough to ask, and her complete happiness. "Mum, I have never been so happy. Conner is like my missing puzzle piece, a piece I didn't realize I was missing. And to be having his baby? It's my dream come true."

"I am truly happy for you, Tina. You know that right?"

"Yeah, I know you are. And it means the world to me that you're here and supporting me."

"Okay, well, let's get to that first bridal shop. And you know, if the one here in Rosebery doesn't have what you want, we can drive into Launceston or even down to Hobart."

"I'm sure I'll find one here in town. I'm just hoping I can find one that fits and doesn't need altering."

Half an hour later, Tina was standing in front of a bank of mirrors in the most gorgeous dress she had ever seen. An ankle length gown made of soft white chiffon. The shop assistant had described it as 'a sleeveless asymmetrical neckline, ruched bodice, sheath pick-up skirt which was pinched with a beaded detail.' The gown flowed over her shoulder, hugging her small breasts and made her feel beautiful. The simple jeweled design on her left hip was stunning with its silvery diamantes and silver thread. There were several thin layers to the skirt, so even with the top couple of layers being pinched up at the waist, her legs were completely covered to her ankles. To make it even better it was the perfect size. As an added bonus, because it was apparently part of last year's collection and it didn't need adjusting, the shop was happy to discount it. Nine hundred dollars seemed like a lot to spend on one dress but her mother had said it was very cheap for a wedding dress and not to worry, as she'd cover it. Tina liked the new leaf her mother had turned over. This day had been more relaxing and easier than any other day they'd ever spent together.

Before Tina came back down to earth from finding the perfect dress, her mother, no, her *mum*, had her in a shoe shop. Within an hour they found the most superb white strappy sandals. They had a cute little kitten heel that she would need to test out while she had her crutches, but she was pretty sure she'd be able to manage. The strap over her toes had an elegant pattern of diamantes, which would match up brilliantly with her dress.

"Well, that was all rather easy. Are you ready for some lunch?"

"Sure am. It might not have taken all that long, but it's made me hungry."

"Yes, that reminds me. We need to drop into a pharmacy on our way too."

Tina grinned like a fool the whole way down the street. Her mum truly had changed it would seem. She hadn't complained once about any of the wedding plans and had seemed genuinely excited about her choice of dress. Intense emotions threatened to have her heart burst from her chest as they entered the pharmacy. She knew she was pregnant and was certain the test would confirm it. She was going to have Conner's baby. If she wasn't stuck in her chair, she'd be jumping up and down and squealing. Well, only if it didn't make her feel ill…

Conner arrived home after Tina. He'd been sure he would be home earlier than this, but he'd become engrossed with the discussions about the Search, and before he knew it the day had gone. It was now past dinnertime as he entered the house searching for Tina.

"Sweetheart? Sorry I'm late. Are you still up?"

With the long summer days, the house was bathed in the low evening light so the fact no lights were on, didn't mean Tina wasn't up and around the place somewhere.

The kitchen was empty, as was the bathroom. He crept down to their bedroom, not wanting to wake her if she was asleep. She had been feeling really tired lately. He'd tried not to worry, did his best to believe her when she said she was just pushing herself at rehab, and was feeling stressed over her future career options.

One step into their bedroom and he stopped short.

"Oh, baby doll. You are gorgeous, and so damn sexy."

His precious mate sat on their bed, her head propped

up on pillows as she read. She laid her book on the bedside cupboard. As she reached over, her dark pink nipple crept just past the edge of the sexy little scrap of lace she was wearing. He knew she hated that her breasts were small, but he loved them. They were high and firm and just right for him to suckle on. The fact she didn't wear a bra most of the time had him permanently aroused just thinking about it.

"Got a present for you."

"So I see."

She chuckled, low and husky, and it sent a shiver the whole way down his spine. "I guess I have a couple presents for you."

He meant to ask how her day went, if she'd found a dress…but his thoughts scattered as he approached the mattress. She'd now thrown back the cover that had hidden her legs and torso and he was all but drooling. Her smooth toned legs were more temptation than he could resist. Quickly pulling his shirt over his head while he kicked off his boots, he bent to run his hands up her calves. As always, she tensed when he got to her knees. She didn't like the scars, Conner didn't like that his mate had suffered so much, but the scars themselves changed nothing about how he felt for her. He kissed each incision point and trailed his tongue up the longer cuts, as he got higher on her thigh.

"Conner, you have to stop. I have. Have to tell you. Something."

Sensing it was important, he pulled away from her

skin with a groan. He prowled up her body so he could kiss her lips as her citrusy scent strengthened with her increasing arousal and enveloped him.

"You look good enough to eat, baby doll. Better make it quick, because I can only resist you for so long. Especially when you dress like this." He flicked his finger over her tight nipple to reinforce his point, but frowned when she hissed and pulled from his touch. What was that about? She'd always liked him flicking her nipples before.

Conner watched as she pulled her other hand from beneath the covers where she'd kept it hidden. In her hand was a long piece of plastic. He cocked an eyebrow at her in question before she turned the plastic over and his heart ceased to beat.

Two. Red. Lines.

Everyone on the planet knew what those two little lines meant.

"We're pregnant?"

At Tina's nod, his heart started again and kicked into high gear. With tears of joy in his eyes, he cupped his mate's face and took her lips in a fevered, passionate kiss.

"You make me so damn happy, Tina. I can't remember ever feeling this complete."

He lowered his head to her breast, where he suckled her tender nipple through the black lace.

"So, you like my new nightie?"

"Hmm, not sure there's enough material to have it

qualify as a nightie…but I certainly like it."

He trailed a finger down each shoulder, taking the straps down her arms. He began purring as she shuddered when her breasts sprung free of the garment. He swiped his tongue over her right nipple before suckling it gently in his mouth as his hands continued to lower the lace down her taut body. He scooted down lower and focused on her still flat tummy. He grinned at the thought that their child was safely growing within. He reverently kissed just above her navel and squeezed his eyes shut against the tears that wanted to escape.

"You are so special, Tina. You've given me so much."

He looked up at her and saw she had tears in her eyes too.

"Don't cry, baby. I didn't mean to make you cry."

"You are. It's only fair I do too. And now I'm pregnant, I'll be more emotional, so you need to get used to tears, honey."

"Baby, I will *never* get used to your tears."

"Well, you'd best distract me then. Maybe removing some more clothing might do the trick."

Conner laughed as he hopped off the bed and stripped out of his pants. He loved when his mate was in a fun mood like she was now. Once naked he stood a moment and looked her over, she was perfect. *How the hell did I ever get so lucky?* She reached her hands over her head and arched her back, offering herself to him. He began purring again. He stripped her nightie off over her feet and tossed the material aside, not caring where it landed.

He crawled between her slender thighs, where he paused to inhale her tangy citrusy scent. It wound through him, filling all the gaps in his soul, completing him. Without blinking, he held her gaze as he lowered and took his first taste of the night. He hummed as the taste exploded across his senses and he went back for more. Her body shuddered beneath him and he splayed a hand over each hip to hold her still so he could continue. One palm landed over her mating mark and the magic sparked through him, as it always did, reminding him she would always be his.

With that thought urging him on, he surged up her body and drove himself into her hot, wet heat. He held still as her muscles rippled and adjusted to his presence within her body. Purring loudly, he lowered his mouth to hers and devoured her. With their tongues dancing he began to move, his strokes starting off long and slow, but he couldn't keep that pace up. He needed his Tina too much. He moved back to kneel, pulling her pelvis up to meet him. He wound his arm around her left thigh carefully, making sure he kept the limb at a comfortable angle for her before he started thrusting deeply into her.

"Hmm, you feel so good."

He felt when Tina was close. Her muscles began to flutter around him. Her arms still stretched above her head gripping the headboard tightly, as her breaths turned to pants. She looked like an angel, her hair a mess of white gold around her flushed face. Arousal stained her cheeks, neck and chest a rosy red beneath the thin film of sweat. Unable to hold back any longer, he threw his head back and roared as he flooded her with his seed. Loving how she went over the edge with him, milking every last drop from him.

Completely spent, he gently lowered her bottom to the bed before he covered her with his much larger body.

"I love you, Tina. More than anything else, I love you."

She gazed up at him, a tender heart breaking smile on her lips. "And you, Conner White, are my whole world. I love you."

She cupped his face in her soft palms and pulled him down to her, claiming his lips along with his heart and soul.

All three he willingly gave her, his mate.

Epilogue

She looked into her mother's serious face as she applied Tina's makeup. So much had happened in the past seven weeks, yet the days had flown by quickly. She'd spent a lot of time with both mothers, plus Adele, getting everything ready. Gloria, Dale, Sophie, Adele and Dominic had also helped her with her rehab. It had been tricky to keep her walking with crutches from Conner. Staying in the chair when she didn't have to drove her nuts some days. But surprising him today with her walking down the aisle was going to be worth every moment. This was definitely going to be a Christmas to remember. All of them, along with Conner, Kelly and Kit had spent the entire previous day transforming the private dining room at Top Pub. Even though the small pub was normally closed on Christmas Day, the owners were opening the private function room especially for them.

Then this morning, the girls had moved onto the chapel where the ceremony was going to be held. Her dad had taken Tina to church every Sunday until she'd moved to Sydney, after that she hadn't been. Gloria always rated her Sunday morning sleep-ins over going to religious services. Conner had been raised with a mix of Christian and Buddhist beliefs. So they were getting married in the Uniting Church with their minister. Conner had brought Tina to a few of their services before today. It was a beautiful old stone building and because their ceremony was going to be in the afternoon it wouldn't mess with their normal Christmas morning service. With the time limitations they hadn't done a lot of decorating. It had to have looked a sight, them all with their hair done and fancy nails tying bows on pews and placing potted poinsettias around the place.

"All those years working the makeup counter at David Jones have finally paid off. You're a masterpiece."

Her mum's words brought her mind back to now. With her makeup done all that was left to do was put her dress on, then it was time for her to get married.

"Thanks, Mum. You look great too. Remi's going to be chasing you around all afternoon."

Her mother blushed and turned away. "Oh, don't be silly." She cleared her throat before standing up from her seat. "Okay, let's get this bride in her dress."

Tina chuckled as she made her way into the other room with her crutches. Remi and Gloria had been inseparable for weeks now. It was sweet to watch, and Remi made sure her mother stuck to her new and improved version of Gloria.

"It's a pity these crutches look so rough. I only need to use one because I'll have either Dad or Conner to lean on but still…"

"Don't worry about it, Tina. Kelly's got it covered."

Tina tilted her head in curiosity. "Kelly has it covered?"

"Sure does, she'll be here soon. But I'm not saying a word till she arrives."

With both her mum and Adele, it didn't take long for Tina to get dressed. She was a little embarrassed that they both saw what she was wearing underneath her dress. Having her mum lace up her white corset was an experience she'd never forget. Man, could that woman giggle like a toddler. Adele had been totally professional about all of it, not only the corset, but the g-string, suspenders and stockings as well.

"Hello?"

Her dad's deep voice rung out through the house.

"In here Dale!" Sophie yelled out before leaving the room.

Tina started to follow but Adele stopped her. "Just wait here a second, *ma chère.*"

Kelly came into the room carrying a stunning 'wedding' crutch.

"Kelly, it's beautiful! Thank you."

She guessed Sophie and Adele played a big part in Kelly's present but Kelly had certainly done a large amount of work too. Conner had introduced the young teen to art and she'd taken to it like a fish to water. She'd been learning airbrushing over the past couple months. This crutch wasn't like the utilitarian ones she was currently using. This one had white leather on the cuff that cupped her arm just below her elbow and on the handle. The metal had been painted white with lightly glittered silver swirls. There were also tiny white silk orchards glued to the bigger swirls. Tina laughed when she noticed there was also a tiny silver leopard charm hanging from the handle. This crutch now looked so elegant and gorgeous that it would fit in perfectly with the wedding theme.

"I wanted to give you something special. I know Uncle Conner is going to be so shocked when you walk down the aisle today."

Leaning her everyday sticks against the wall, Tina pulled Kelly in for a light hug. She didn't want to get either of them wrinkled. Adele and Kelly were her attendants. They each wore a simple knee-length red sundress. Sophie and Jake rushed in with all their flowers.

"The cars are all here so we need to get a move on but you ladies need your flowers first."

Adele and Kelly both had small bouquets of blood-red roses with small white orchids. Tina had the same thing, just slightly bigger.

"Oh my, you three look so lovely." Sophie paused to look over at Tina's mum, "Gloria? Let's get a move on so we get there in plenty of time to see my son pass out."

Chuckling the whole way, Sophie and her mum headed out the door. Jake was driving Tina and her attendants, so he promptly left to go warm up the car. Adele and Kelly headed off to get what they needed to take with them, leaving Tina a much needed moment alone.

Not much later, a throat clearing had Tina turning around. Her father stood there, looking uncomfortable in his suit and tie.

"Wow, Dad. You scrub up nicely for an old man." She winked at her dad as he nervously laughed.

"Not half as good as you do. You look amazing, Tina. Conner is a lucky man."

"I'm a lucky woman."

"Tina, I can't tell you what it means to me to see you looking so happy. You've turned into an exceptional young woman. One I'm proud to call my daughter."

"Thanks, Dad. I love you too. But please don't get emotional. These pregnancy hormones have me crying all the time, and even though Mum assures me my mascara is waterproof, I'd rather not test it just yet."

"Yeah, well, I'm not real good with emotions either. I just wanted to give you this before we head off to the church."

Her dad pulled a strand of pearls from his pocket.

"These go way back in my mother's family. Not sure exactly how old they are. But I can tell you, your mother, grandmother and great grandmother wore them on their wedding days. Thankfully I put them in a safety deposit box at the bank so they didn't get lost in the fire."

Blinking back tears, Tina unclasped the necklace Conner had given her all those months ago and allowed her father to fasten the pearl strand around her neck. The cool weight felt good against her skin. She looked down to the gold heart with its little paw print wondering how she could include it in her outfit.

"I have an idea that might work, if you still want to wear it. I know how special it is to you."

"I would really like to have it with me today. What's your idea?"

Her father took the new shorter chain she'd bought for it and proceeded to wrap it around her right wrist twice. It hung loosely but not so loose it would fall off.

"Perfect. So the pearls cover my something old. Mum gave me these emerald earrings, so that's the new. The innersoles of my sandals are blue, so that's covered. What else? Something borrowed…"

Adele came in cutting her off. "Borrowed is easy."

They were getting ready at Dominic and Adele's house so Adele grabbed up one of Kelly's flower clips and carefully added it to her hair. "There. All done. Now, let's get this bride to the altar on time."

Conner flexed his neck, moving his head from side to side. His palms were sweaty and he couldn't keep his feet still.

Or his hands.

"Stop fidgeting, bro. She'll be here any minute now. You know brides have to be late. Apparently, it's in some rule book woman have."

Conner appreciated Dom's attempt to cheer him up but it didn't work. The sound of high heels on the tiled entrance brought his head up. He knew it couldn't be Tina. The music hadn't started yet. But he couldn't resist the pull to watch. His heart skipped a beat as Gloria, followed closely by Remi, entered and made their way to the front row. They sat near Jennifer, who made sure a space was left for Dale. As father of the bride, he was walking Tina down the aisle. His mum came in soon after and came up to give both him and Dom a kiss before taking her place on the front pew. *If the mothers are here, Tina has to be on her way.*

Minutes later the church hushed as the first notes of 'You Are The Wind Beneath My Wings' floated over the space from the keyboardist sitting to the side of the church.

"Ahh, look at my girl. Damn she looks so good now, doesn't she?"

"That she does, Dom."

Conner watched as Kelly walked up the aisle toward them. She had the biggest smile on her face as she slowly stepped up the red carpet. Her black curls were mostly up in a fancy knot high on her head. There were half dozen curls loose, hanging down around her upturned face. The red sundress was a little Christmassy without going over the top. She winked at him and Dom before she stood to the side and looked back down the aisle.

Conner heard Dom suck in his breath as Adele came up the aisle in a similar dress to Kelly, proudly holding a bouquet of red roses, and some little white things—orchids maybe—in front of her as she did the bridal march. She blew Dominic a kiss and winked at him before taking a place next to Kelly.

"What's with all the winking?"

"You'll see soon enough, Conner. Here she comes. Hope you're ready for this."

What the hell was Dom on about? He'd been ready to marry Tina since the first time he'd spoken with her.

Loud gasps from the back rows brought his attention from staring at Dom to the back of the church.

Conner's eyes burned with unshed tears.

His heart froze.

And his knees went weak.

He threw an arm out and caught Dom's shoulder to keep himself upright.

"She's walking. My angel is walking."

"She sure is."

Conner couldn't believe his eyes. His Tina was walking down the aisle. *Walking*. She held a crutch in one hand and had the other wound around Dale's arm. As she walked closer toward him, he saw how lovingly her gown fitted her. It was perfect for her. The skirt was light and floated around her ankles, but fell close enough to her legs that it didn't tangle with her feet or the crutch. Her flowers were the same as the girls, just a bigger bunch. Her hair was a series of intricate plaits all woven into a pattern starting high on her head and he assumed trailed down her back. Half her hair wasn't up but hung straight down like liquid gold over her shoulders. She was breathtaking. Dominic chuckled quietly by his side.

"Come on, bro. Pull yourself together. She's nearly here."

"She's walking."

"Yeah, I can see that."

"She's magnificent."

"Well, go marry her then."

Somehow Conner managed to take a step forward as Dale and Tina stopped. Dale took the flowers from Tina, and Adele stepped forward to take them. He then took Tina's hand in his and placed it in Conner's outstretched one.

"I'm trusting you to keep looking after my daughter, Conner. And I expect you to love her forever, son."

"Yes, sir. That's my plan."

With a nod, Dale stepped back and from that moment all Conner saw was Tina.

"Surprise."

That one whispered word melted his heart. She'd obviously been hiding the fact that she'd come so far in her rehab. Just so she could surprise him now.

"I want to kiss you so much."

He was rewarded with a lopsided grin. "You'll have to wait another few minutes."

The minister chose that moment to begin the service. Not that Conner heard it. He couldn't tear his focus from Tina. He managed to snap out of his trance enough to slide Tina's wedding ring on her finger and say 'I do'. Then finally the words he'd been waiting for, "You may kiss the bride."

Taking her face between his palms, he leaned in and took possession of her mouth. All their guests cheered loudly and began wolf whistling as he took his time exploring his wife's mouth.

"C'mon, bro. You need to come up for air."

Conner growled low as he pulled away from Tina. He gazed into her dilated eyes as he noticed her lips part to pant for breath.

"Save it for the honeymoon!"

He suspected it was Kit who had yelled out and he laughed as a rosy blush spread over Tina's cheeks and she began chuckling. He turned, and Tina took her flowers back from Adele before she linked arms with him. They made their way over to a table and signed the certificates before they walked back down the aisle, and Conner felt like his cheeks were going to crack from how wide his grin was. He was the luckiest man alive.

She was now Tina White.

Wife to Conner White.

She turned to watch her husband as the entrees were served. She'd selected the menu with great care and now waited for her husband's reaction. He looked down then straight over to her.

"Is this quail?"

Tina picked up the menu and read the description, "*Rannoch Farm quail half, pistachio nut and veal farce, wrapped with mild pancetta and served with nashi pear chutney. Why? I thought cats liked to eat small birds.*"

Just like she wanted, Conner roared out a laugh and moved to kiss her. "I love your sense of humor, baby doll. Although, I'm not sure I'm brave enough to see what's coming for the main course."

"Personally I can't wait."

They continued their lighthearted banter as they ate their meal. Once she was finished, she cast a look over all their guests. She nudged Conner when she saw Remi feed her mum from his fork.

"Oh, that is too adorable."

"It is pretty sweet. You weren't around when Remi first came here. He'd been searching for Adele for over twenty years. He was a shell of a man, but within days of finding his long lost daughter, he'd packed up and moved from France to here. He began to live life again as he got to know Adele and Kelly but your mum has been the one to truly make him smile. Huh, looks like your dad is getting lucky in love too. Must be something in the air."

He turned to nuzzle her neck as she glanced over to where her dad sat with his arm draped around Jennifer's shoulders as they both ate and chatted to each other with a soft look in their eyes.

"I've been wondering about something."

"It seems I've managed to keep you wondering about a few things tonight."

Tina felt rather proud of herself. She'd managed to keep so many things a surprise for her new husband.

"Indeed you have. And I'm really looking forward to finding out each and every one. But this second, it's the name holders that have me puzzled. Why a glass slipper?"

"You do recall the whole Cinderella thing don't you?"

Conner briefly closed his eyes as he shook his head with a chuckle. "Yeah, I remember. So, tonight, am I your Prince Charming or your knight in shining armor?"

"Well, it is our wedding. I certainly hope you don't need to do any rescuing here. So tonight, you're neither. Tonight, you're my noble guardian."

Dominic suddenly rose to his feet, tapping his glass to get everyone's attention.

"I do believe it's that time of the evening for me to say my bit. And I can't listen to them get mushy with each other any longer. So best man speech it is!"

Everybody had a good chuckle, as Dominic no doubt planned, before he continued on with his speech.

"Let me begin by saying just how stunning Tina looks tonight. To see her walk down that aisle was amazing. Some of you might not realize that before today Tina's been in a wheelchair recovering from a badly injured leg. She's been rather sneaky, and I'm not ashamed to admit, I helped in her attempts to pull the wool over my little brother's eyes. You see, Tina's been walking with sticks for a while now. But she wanted to keep it as a wedding surprise for Conner. A special gift from her to him on this special day."

"You were in on it too? How many people did you recruit, baby doll?"

"As many as I needed. I wanted to see your face as I

walked down the aisle to you. It was worth every moment."

Conner held her gaze with his as Dominic continued with his speech. Conner didn't say a word but the look in his eyes said it all. She could see he was filled with love for her. She'd never tire from seeing that look.

The sound of everyone applauding snapped them from their intimate moment and she blushed at having missed Dominic's speech. She was sure he'd tease her about it later.

"Well, c'mon, get out on the dance floor. First dance time."

Tina squealed in surprise as Conner scooped her up out of her chair and headed to the dance floor to the sound of laughter and applause. He slid her down his body as the first notes of Savage Garden's 'I Knew I Loved You' came over the speakers. Holding her close to him, he took her weight so they easily glided around the floor as the lyrics rolled out through the room.

"Hmm, so you 'dreamed me into life' did you?"

Conner whispered close to her ear and she felt warmth spread throughout her body.

"I thought the lyrics were perfect for us."

"They certainly are. I definitely loved you before I met you."

Tina sung a couple lines quietly so only Conner could hear her.

"*A thousand angels dance around you, I am complete now that I've found you.*"

She saw the gleam of tears in his eyes as she blinked back her own. He was so beautiful. She put a palm to his face and caressed his cheek. "I love you, my husband."

His smile was both breathtaking and heart breaking as he lifted her up in the air and kissed her. "And I love you, my wife."

The song finished and Dominic's voice announced the father daughter dance. Her dad swaggered up to her and spoke in a voice rough with emotion.

"May I have this dance?"

The first notes of 'I Loved Her First' by Heartland came on as her dad took her hand and pulled her into his arms. He'd asked for this song. Aside from the beautiful pearls she wore, it had been his only request, so naturally she'd given it to him. Now as the lyrics played through her mind she couldn't stop the tears that flowed. Just as she'd done with Conner, her father leaned close to her ear and softly sung a few lines, *"and a place in my heart will always be hers, from the first breath she breathed."*

Tina enjoyed holding her father close as they twirled around the dance floor for the rest of the country song. Memories of good times she'd had as a child with her dad flooded her mind. Him pushing her on the swing in their backyard, the same swing Conner had sat on with her. Taking her swimming at the beach in the summer, and the way he'd played in the surf with her, making sure she laughed for the best part of the day. Then newer memories surged forward, him rushing into her Sydney hospital room, panic written clearly in his features. He'd crumpled beside her bed as he clutched her hand to his mouth. He'd been heartbroken for her. His love for her obvious, even though they hadn't seen each other for so long. She tightened her arms around him as the song ended.

"Thank you, Dad. For everything, but mostly, for always loving me."

"Oh, sweet pea, keep that up and you'll have me in tears. You'll always be my girl, and I'll always love you. Now, your man's looking edgy, and you'd best reassure him you're crying happy tears."

Carefully wiping her eyes with a tissue her dad pressed into her hand, Tina allowed her dad to help her walk over to Conner. Tucked into her husband's warm, hard body, they danced away until Dominic announced it was time for dinner to be served. Connor again swept her off her feet and carried her to their seats.

"You realize I can walk now?"

"And do you realize I will always want to carry you?"

As they reached their table, plates were set down before their seats. Tina felt the laugh begin in Conner's tummy before it rumbled up his throat and he threw his head back as the sound escaped his mouth.

"Whole baked trout? Let me guess, because all cats like fish?"

"That may have had something to do with it."

She felt her cheeks heat with embarrassment as she realized everyone was watching them. She looked out over all their guests. It was easy to pick who knew about the shifters. Those who didn't were looking confused while everyone else had a knowing smile.

"I'm not sure I want to know what you have planned for dessert, sweetheart."

She chuckled as he lowered her into her seat. "Well, I couldn't think of anything dessert wise so we just have chocolate soufflé—but it is going to be served with cream."

"Well, you do know how much this cat likes his cream."

Conner had whispered directly in her ear and heat settled between her thighs. Oh yeah, she knew… Conner took a sharp intake of breath, before groaning. She smiled as she knew he could smell her arousal.

"Some days having a really good sense of smell can be a curse. How long until we can leave?"

Conner looked down at his mate and wife. Tina had her arms around his neck as she laughed. He held her against his bare chest. She looked resplendent in her emerald green bikini. He'd searched online for hours to find one that looked just like the one she'd worn in their first dream.

"I should have known we'd end up at Bondi Beach for our honeymoon, especially after you gave me my bikini this morning."

"You're not the only one full of surprises, baby doll."

Conner thought back to their wedding night. He'd watched as she unzipped her dress and allowed it to fall free from her body. He just about swallowed his tongue when he saw what was revealed. White stockings held up by a lacy garter belt covered her legs. A stunning white corset wrapped her torso and pushed up her breasts. Unable to resist, he'd pulled her to him, intent on getting her naked but she'd had different ideas. With a seductive smile she shook her head and moved to undo his pants. After pushing them over his hips, she pressed his shoulders until he sat on the edge of the bed. Naked from the waist down to his ankles, where his pants remained bunched above his shoes. He'd watched in awe as she gracefully lowered herself to kneel between his thighs. She'd then held his gaze as she lowered until the head of his steel-hard erection was surrounded by the soft wet heat of her mouth. The things she'd done with her tongue had driven him to the edge of sanity. Feeling himself stiffen and lengthen at the memories, he pulled himself free and focused on Tina. She now had a red hue to her cheeks, as if she had been remembering the same thing.

Recalling the reason he'd brought her here, that first dream they'd shared, he gave her a sly smile before he ran for the water. She squealed and clung tighter as they plunged into the cool ocean. It was mid afternoon on the twenty-sixth of December and the cool water was a welcome treat on the hot Australian summer day. He refused to release her until he was in deeper water. When he was waist deep, he halted and lowered her to her feet. Returning his sly smile, she stepped away from him. Laughing loudly, she fell back sinking below the surface.

Diverting from the dream, he dived in next to her and came up with her back in his arms. He wasn't sure she'd be able to push herself up like she'd done in the dream. He spun her around before lowering his mouth to hers. "I believe I promised I'd never stop doing this."

The water was crowded so Conner moved to the shore and headed toward the lifeguard tower. He had a plan. He found a spot at the rear of the tower and lowered to the sand with her still in his grip.

"You remember."

"Yeah, I remember everything about our dreams, baby doll."

Tears welled in her eyes. "I'm sorry. So sorry I didn't believe you."

"It's okay, Tina. You were dealing with so much and I threw in snow leopard shifters and dreams that are real—no wonder you didn't believe it all. That's not why we're here. I brought you to this spot to focus on what we have now. To close the door on all that pain and to move forward with me and our baby." He put a palm over her tummy. There was a slight bump there now, a tangible sign of the life growing within.

Tina took his face in her palms, bringing his gaze to hers. "I already shut that door, Conner. Mating with you, finding out about our baby then getting married—that door is welded shut. It's not ever opening again. My depression is completely gone now. But I will keep seeing Jennifer for a while, professionally, to make sure I stay well with the pregnancy hormones. Although, I suspect I'll be seeing her personally for a very long time."

Conner chuckled. "Yeah, I think you might be right there. Jennifer and Dale look rather settled with each other."

"And Mum and Remi equally so."

"Yep."

He allowed her to pull him down to her parted lips where he delved in to taste his wife and mate. He shuddered as her scent intensified with her arousal. After devouring her mouth, he moved to feather kisses down her throat. She moaned in response before whispering the plea he'd been waiting for.

"I really think we should head back to the hotel."

Scooping her back up in his arms, he strode off toward their hotel as fast as he could without giving away he wasn't fully human. "I couldn't agree more, baby doll."

The next installment of Fire and Snow is Guardian's Shadow, which tells Jesse and Kit's journey and will be available soon.